the boys i've loved and the end of the world

catarine hancock

Cover by Gaylen Bailey.
Interior Art by Brooke Aschenbrenner.

ISBN: 978-1548053970

to all young writers and poets

it has taken me a long time to develop my writing style. when i first started writing poetry, shortly before i entered high school, my poems were full of clichés and every line oozed unoriginality. it took me several months, nearly a year, before i really began to get a feel for writing prose and poetry. even now, after four years, i am still changing and growing as a writer.

my message to you is to not give up. if your work seems cliché or boring, keep writing. if nobody seems to like it, keep writing. even when you have writer's block and nothing you write is decent, keep writing. that is how you grow.

emily dickinson did not stop writing. sara teasdale did not stop writing. robert frost and edgar allen poe did not stop writing. pablo neruda, maya angelou, e.e. cummings, langston hughes; these are our predecessors. and as for the poets who come after us: we are theirs.

something i have learned through sharing my writing is that oftentimes, your writing will never be good enough in your eyes. you will always find something missing. it is very rare that you will write something that will make you say, "there is nothing i would add to this. it has portrayed everything i have wanted it to."

but that doesn't mean it isn't good enough in the eyes of somebody else. to somebody else, that poem, that piece of prose, could be exactly what they are feeling. it could resonate with them. it could make them *feel*.

and that, above all else, is the most important part of writing. if you write with feeling, and if you can make somebody else smile, or cry, or think, then you have succeeded.

i hope that i have succeeded, just as i hope you will too.

for my followers.
you have given me more than i could have ever asked
for.
thank you.

to the first
i was full of words
and you were the one
who cut deep enough
to unleash them.

not a day goes by
that i don't thank you
for it.

-c.h.

i didn't think this needed an explanation
but i'm going to explain it
anyway

i write about love
because it is
what i know
i write about pain
because it is
what i've felt
i write about abuse
because it is
what i've been through
i write about politics
because it is
what i care about

i write about
what i have
experienced
i write about
what makes me
quake with anger
heave with sadness
smile with joy

i will never write
for anybody
but myself

i will never write
something that
i don't mean

i know my art
will not reach everybody
and i have never

expected it to

but i expect—
no
i *demand*—
respect as an artist
because that
is what
i deserve

-c.h.

eclipse
we looked at each other like
we were the sun and the moon
locked in a gravitational war,
bound to cross and bound to
break apart.

to you,
i was the entire night sky.
to me,
you were just another
forlorn stargazer.

but you looked at me like
i was your whole universe.
i cried because i was
full of dead stars and broken debris,
but you still called me
beautiful.

you were the flaming meteor
about to send me up in smoke
but i kissed you anyways.

there's a burning crater on my lips
from your touch and
i think i may always be in love
with you.

we looked at each other like
we were the sun and the moon
and we knew we'd only eclipse for so long.

we knew all along that
soon we would be apart,
just waiting for gravity to bring us back together
again.

                                    -c.h

you're the only one who doesn't haunt me
i think i saw you in my dreams, my dear,
it brought us back to the time,
when life was far less complicated,
and you would say, "you're mine."

you were by far the only one i loved,
but that was way back then,
for we walked on a long old rope
that was paper, paper thin.

it snapped and sent us falling down,
i felt you slip away from me,
but that's okay, for when i landed,
there was something beautiful to see.

i saw the gold around my feet
and the darkness up above;
sometimes the key to joy
is falling out of love.

i think i saw you in my dreams, my dear,
and i learned a thing or two,
i have a soulmate, he's there somewhere,
but that soulmate isn't you.

                                        -c.h.

us pertaining to a rainbow

red: when i first met you, all i saw was the red of your shirt and the plumpness of your lips, and the first thing i thought was *i want you, i want you, i want you.* you asked for my name and i blushed bright red, you looked at me and said *oh god, i want you, i want you, i want you*, or at least you said it in your head, because i swear i saw it in your eyes.

orange: your touch burned me like fire and i couldn't get away from your scorching heat no matter how hard i tried and *god, did i love it.* you tasted sour and sweet at the same time, but nothing tasted as good or sizzled as much as when you first kissed me.

yellow: euphoria fell short of describing me when you were there and my laughter would bubble over from my lips, and you made me so *happy.* i would trace my fingers across your jaw because you glowed, oh my, you glowed like a sun and to me, you were the equivalent of a star.

green: we were blossoming and ever changing, but we walked to each other's heartbeats and i could feel you wrapping around me like a vine, but i didn't even notice they were crushing me until they were roped around my lungs.

blue: i woke up the next morning with bruises on my face and fingerprints around my throat, but it was all metaphorical because while your hands never touched me that night, your words slapped me as if they had. i spent the day hiding from you in the bathtub, afraid to look in the mirror, for i knew i was decaying.

indigo: you didn't pick up your phone that night when i tried to call you while you were at work, and you didn't come home until one in the morning, and i shouldn't have over thought it, but it's hard to over think something that's written all over the walls and in this case, written in lipstick on your neck.

violet: you handed me my suitcase one sunday morning and told me to pack my things, and i thought this was god's punishment to me for not believing, because maybe if i had gone to church that day the inevitable would have been delayed a little bit longer. i asked you twelve more times if you were sure you wanted me to leave, but all you did was stare at me with shadows under your eyes, because maybe, i had been sucking the brightness out of you all this time, too.

black: i left months ago, and i am still haunted by you at night, even if i close my eyes and pretend that i'm not here anymore. the only place i ever dreamt of being was by your side, and now that that dream is crushed, what is there left to want, and even after all this time, *i still want you, i still want you, i still want you.*

-c.h.

rule #1: never cry over a fuckboy (how to get over someone in a month and a half)

week one: rinse your body of his touch. drown yourself in hot water from the shower, choke on the steam that rises from your red, soaking flesh. scrub yourself raw, until you have shed every last skin cell that could have been touched by his fingertips.

week two: take his jacket and drench it in gasoline. light fire to it in the middle of the night, let the smoke swirl in your lungs. inhale, exhale, the smell of him is leaving. leave the burnt remains on his doorstep.

week three: get drunk, turn off your phone, so you won't be able to call him. leave it in the other room. watch sit-coms and soap operas until four in the morning. laugh and cry until you throw up. it won't be because of him.

week four: hold the necklace he bought you close to your chest. remember. you can remember the good so long as you don't forget the bad. break the clasp with a hammer and place it back in its velvet box.

week five: buy yourself a new dress. put it on and call the boy who's been chasing you since grade school, ask him if he wants to go out. he'll say yes. take him to dinner and hold his hand, but do not kiss. adjust. adjust slowly, carefully.

week six: call him. when he picks up, ask him how he's doing. when he says he's doing fine, tell him you're glad. when he asks why, tell him you were just checking and hang up without a goodbye. he will call back that night, and the next, and the next. but he already lost you, and you are okay.

-c.h.

bias
when i am talking
to a boy and he finds out
that i write poetry,
the first thing he asks is,

"will you ever write about me?"

i tell him honestly,
"hopefully, i won't."

and he asks,
"why?"

it's my answer that
always catches them.

"because,
if i end up writing about you,
it means that all the promises
you made me
ended up being broken
and maybe you're somebody
i shouldn't have spent so much
time on
if all you were going to do
in the end is
break my heart."

if they're smart,
they call me on it.
tell me that every
relationship is worth it
because you always have
something to learn.

in the end,

these are the boys
i write about most.

but if they love me,
they stay quiet.
because the thought
of them breaking my heart
is enough to suck the
words from their tongues.

these are the boys
i don't write about.
not because they aren't there,
but because i cast the
fatal blow.

and even now,
i have never been good
at saying sorry.

-c.h

oceans, the future
i watch the brown waves
stumble against the shore.
the water sloshes against
my shins, hot and oily.

plastic bags wrap around
my ankles
like seaweed,
bottle caps crunch
under my toes;
the new seashell.

i walk along the
glass-bedded sand
and trace my feet
through soda tabs.

a turtle limps by,
its neck strangled
by a six pack ring.

i am so thrilled
to see an animal,
i don't even notice
it can barely breathe.

-c.h.

for the girls with the frizzy hair and bitten nails and the boys with bushy eyebrows and marionette limbs:

1. there will be the kids with perfect skin and white smiles and flawless bodies. do not be scared of them. often the "prettiest" people are the most hurt inside.

2. find a home away from home for yourself, whether it be the gym floor, the computer lab, or the auditorium stage. you will need one.

3. let your heart get broken. you have to learn how to breathe with pieces of your heart piercing your lungs. trust somebody you shouldn't, make a bad decision. but always learn from your mistakes. too many wrong moves will kill you.

4. there will always be somebody out to get you. don't let them.

5. in every school, there is one teacher that you will connect with more than any other. cherish that bond, because it only comes once, and you only have so much time.

6. don't wear that dress if it doesn't feel right. don't wear that shirt if you don't actually like it. don't do anything you don't want to do for the sake of staying with the trends.

7. for the girls: if somebody touches you in a way you don't like, don't be afraid to fight back. you are not weak. you are not an object. make sure they, and you, know that. make sure your fellow girls know their worth, too, and do not contribute to the degradation of it.

8. for the boys: if you see a girl in trouble, help her. make sure she doesn't go into that bedroom alone with him while she's drunk. stand up for her if she's being harassed. if you see something but can't do anything yourself; tell somebody. call the police. protect girls, and educate your fellow boys on how to treat them.

9. watch the news. read the paper. engage in discussion. know about politics and what's going on in the world. in times like these, it's no longer alright to not care about things; in fact, it could be harmful.

10. people will die. people you know, people your peers know. car wrecks, drugs, suicides, gun violence: they will all take people you walk those halls with. so, that being said: if you love somebody, tell them. if you think somebody may need a friend, be that friend. you don't want to be stuck in the aftermath of a tragedy, thinking, "oh, if only i'd said this. if only i'd done this."

11. there will be days where you look in the mirror and want to remold your body like clay, days where you may not even want to get out of bed. on those days, it's okay to cry, to want to be different. but the next morning, remind yourself; you will be okay, you will be okay, you will be okay.

-c.h.

time is everything
it's been 61 days since you last told me you loved me. 1,464 hours,
or 87,840 minutes, or 5,270,400 seconds. i have never been one to
keep time but i used to count the hours we talked to each other on the
phone (the record was 5) and how many seconds it took for you to
tell me you loved me (sometimes it was .65 seconds, but when you
were feeling sad it was 3.8), and how many minutes you spent
staring at me in class (one time it was a whole 12 minutes before the
teacher called on you). i have been alive for 15 years, or 5,475 days,
and you were a part of my life for only 102. 2,448 hours, or 146,880
minutes, or 8,812,800 seconds. i have never been one to keep time
but i wanted to keep track of us. now i only keep a record of how
long i go without thinking of you (5.4 minutes) and how many hours
i spend crying because you're gone (so far: 73). i have never been
one to keep time but i wanted to count how many days (64) i was in
love with you and now i have to count how many days i'm going to
hurt because you left (forever).

-c.h.

the boys i've loved and the end of the world #1
"the world is ending, you know."

he looks at me through tired eyes as i say it. "is that why you're here?"

i shrug. "i guess." he takes a pack of cigarettes out of his pocket and smiles when i raise my eyebrows. "i didn't know you smoke, now," i say.

"i don't," he explains as he places one between his lips, "but the world is ending. can't get lung cancer in twelve days."

i chuckle, watch him take his first drag from his first cigarette. he coughs, and smiles at me. "i loved you, you do know that, right?"

"yeah, yeah, i know," i reply, and he takes a longer drag this time.

"you were important… an important lesson, i think."

"how so?"

"we were too young, too stupid. we were incapable of fixing the mess we'd made with our own two hands. only time could do that."

he nods, smoke filtering from his parted lips. the moon turns his black hair to a silvery blue, and i am almost caught up in how beautiful he could be, sometimes.

"how many times did you fall in love with her before you realized she would never give you what you wanted?" i ask, and he blinks, surprised by the question.

"the same goes for you," he counters, "but with me instead."

there is a comfortable silence. "twice," i say, finally, "what about you?"

"twice. and it was always after you. it was always what ruined us, again and again."

i think about this as he finishes his cigarette. "sometimes, i wonder if we could have made it. if we weren't so young," i tell him.

he nods his head, smiles. "yeah, sometimes i think about that too."

-c.h.

tomorrow

the sink in the kitchen won't stop dripping. when i sit on the living room couch i can hear it over the hum of the television and i think i've told you to fix it four times. every time you smile and tell me you will tomorrow. that's what you've always said. "i'll mop the floor-- tomorrow. i'll mow the yard-- tomorrow. i'll stop you from crying-- tomorrow." i'm beginning to think that you are just an endless closet of throw-away promises and old shoes that you used to wear when you liked to chase me. once you caught me, you took them off and never put them back on because you knew you'd never need to. they sit in the closet next to a pile of "tomorrow"'s and i don't let you see me cry anymore. you've long since forgotten how to make me stop.

the sink in the kitchen keeps dripping and it keeps me up at night. i once believed that our house was too small for the size of us but i can feel the cold seeping in from the corners because this house is empty. it has cobwebs inside the cupboards and dust bunnies under the bed; they keep our secrets company. i never told you how afraid i was to lose you-- i tried and you shook your head and said "tomorrow." tomorrow. tomorrow.

maybe tomorrow will be better, i tell myself, maybe tomorrow you will clean the gutters, maybe tomorrow you will fix the sink, maybe tomorrow you will love me again; i've been told that you begin to develop the habits of the ones you love and i've started adding my "tomorrow"'s to the pile in the closet. they've covered your old shoes and you've forgotten what it was like to love me, and the sink in the kitchen won't stop dripping but it still works. you still come home every day, you barely talk to me, but you still come home.

i look at you, and i think about tomorrow. tomorrow. tomorrow. maybe tomorrow you won't come home. maybe i hope, deep down, that tomorrow, you won't. maybe eventually, these will be "tomorrow"'s that i won't add to the pile in the closet. there are pictures of us hung above the fireplace, and the mantle is covered with dust. the sink in the kitchen still drips, but i say "i love you" anyway. i hope you'll love me too, tomorrow.

-c.h.

children's games
i am tired of playing
these childhood games with you

you run too fast
and i can never reach you
for i am tired of chasing
someone who will never let
me catch them

you've always been good at hiding
but you're invisible to me
and it seems that you don't understand
the pain of losing someone and not being able
to find them again

you aren't one for following rules
and i know this because
no matter how many times i get
"he loves me"
when i pluck petals off
you always find a way for it to be
"he loves me not"

-c.h.

this is me confessing that i'm still in love with you
i hope you think of me.
i hope you think of the slope of my nose and the arch in my brows.
i hope you think of the rise and fall of my chest with every breath i took, how i breathed for you.
it was all for you.
i hope you think of the wrinkles in the corners of my eyes when i smiled, and i hope you think of how i'll never smile at you again.
i hope it hurts.
i hope the syllables of my name are printed in black ink on your tongue and i hope she sees the mark i left on you, oh no it may not have been good but by god it is permanent.
i hope her name feels out of place between your teeth because you were so used to saying mine.
you see, from the very beginning i wanted to engrave myself into you, i wanted to embed my signature with melted gold and red lipstick, i wanted it to look pretty, but we were over so fast i had to scratch it into your chest with my hands.
i still have your blood encrusted beneath my fingernails, like i still have the shreds of our Polaroid pictures that i never quite grew angry enough to throw away.
i hope you haven't let go of me yet. please don't let go of me.
i hope you think of me, because all i do, is think of you.

-c.h.

ode to the lgbt+ community
i am lgbt+ and proud.
i am part of a community
that has struggled its entire
existence, so people know that
it exists. but we are still here,
and we are so strong.

i am gay and proud.
i have fought against other
men who are insecure in their
masculinity, who view two men
holding hands as a threat
and not something beautiful.

i am lesbian and proud.
i have battled the stereotypes
and fetishization of who i am
because i am not a mold
and i am not something to
jack off to: i am a human.

i am bisexual and proud.
i continue to scream that
i am not in a phase
and i am not whatever sexuality
fits with whoever i'm dating,
and i am just as valid as you are.

i am transgender and proud.
i was born in the wrong body
but that doesn't make me any
less human, and it terrifies me that
people would rather kill us than
let us become who we're meant to be.

i am asexual and proud.

i have pushed back against
the idea that i am an emotionless
robot; i have feelings and emotions
just like you. why does not having
sexual desire mean i'm incapable of love?

i am genderqueer and proud.
i don't fit into the spectrum
and sometimes i lean more
in one direction than the other,
but i am know who i am,
even if you don't understand it.

i am pansexual and proud.
i am as valid as bisexuality,
but ever so different; i fall in love
with people with no regard for
their gender, they could be male,
female, or somewhere in between.

i am aromantic and proud.
i have worked to dismantle
the belief that i cannot have
meaningful relationships;
i may not fall in love as easily,
but i do love people, just not romantically.

i am an ally and proud.
i have marched alongside them
since stonewall, since the AIDS epidemic,
since DOMA, since the pulse shooting,
and i will march alongside them
until they no longer need me to.

i am lgbt+ and proud.
i am lgbt+ and valid.
i am lgbt+ and human.

-c.h.

recipe for disaster (layer cake)

LAYER ONE: Place 3 awkward glances, 2 shy half-smiles, and 1 clumsy introduction in a bowl. Stir haphazardly and add 4 cups of nerves and 9 tablespoons of awe. Allow ingredients to settle, then combine 75 minutes of get-to-know-you conversation and 1 1/2 cups of coffee and heat for 30 seconds. Add mixture to other bowl and mix thoroughly. Sprinkle 2 freshly exchanged phone numbers and 1 excited goodbye on top. Bake for 25 minutes. Lay on cake dish.

LAYER TWO: In another bowl, prepare 9,143 text messages, 226 phone calls, and 33 dates. Place 7 romance movies, 4 chick-flicks, 8 comedies, and 2 tear-jerkers in mixing cup and melt in microwave. Slice 3 Italian, 3 Mexican, and 6 fast food restaurants into strips and coat each in 2 nights spent throwing up because of food poisoning. Combine all ingredients and stir thoroughly. Bake for 25 minutes. Stack on top of layer one.

LAYER THREE: Dump 2 other girls, 12 fights, and 15 bottles of alcohol and don't stir. Crack open 2 hearts and pour contents into sink, place the shells in with the mixture. Dice 2 failing attempts at leaving and 1 final success at getting out into cubes and combine with 4 bruises on the right cheek and a set of finger marks around the throat. Heat up 5 cups of tears and combine all ingredients. Stir until chunky. Bake for 25 minutes. Stack on top of layer two.

ICING: Combine 1,646 "I love you"'s, 20,310 kisses, 2 sets of hands, 5 necklaces, 3 ties, 1 dress shirt, 7 times under the sheets, 2 times in the shower, and 1 time in a club bathroom. Add in a squirt of heartfelt promises and sincere apologies. Mix and then spread on top of cake.

Serves: two lonely people.

-c.h.

this is how they kill us

you are beautiful they gushed as they tucked in your shirt because they thought it looked better that way, *you are beautiful* they complimented as they switched out your nail polish color to something they liked, *you are beautiful* they delivered as they watched the hairdresser take scissors to your hair and chop it off in chunks because they wanted it shorter, *you are beautiful* they snapped as they cleaned out your closet to give you new clothes because your older clothes weren't up to style, *you are beautiful* they groaned as they took away your candy because it was your fifth piece, *you are beautiful* they cursed as they took away your eyeliner because they didn't like how you wore it, *you are beautiful* they accused as they forced you to exercise way longer than you could handle because they thought you weren't athletic enough, *you are beautiful* they screamed as they pointed in disgust at your stomach because they thought it was too big, *you are beautiful* they sobbed as they found you crying in the shower after they said you were worthless earlier that night, *you are beautiful* they begged as they held your hand in the hospital bed because you'd swallowed too many pills, *you were beautiful* they whispered as they watched your coffin lower into the ground because you are dead and *you are beautiful.*

-c.h.

ten words for the ten boys i've kissed
1. i've forgotten how your lips taste. i'll never forget you.
2. i didn't love you, and you deserved more than me.
3. maybe if you weren't a homophobe, it could've worked out.
4. people said you were gay, and i cared too much.
5. you made me laugh more than cry. i cried lots.
6. thank you for reminding me how to love myself; i'd forgotten.
7. i thought you were my soulmate. i guess people change.
8. you were wild. i wasn't. something kept me coming back.
9. you used to love me. you didn't when we kissed.
10. i could kiss you for the rest of my life.

-c.h.

anchor

the weight of us is so heavy.
we chain ourselves to cement blocks--
they are the promises we make.

i jumped into the ocean
for you when i could not swim--
but you did not follow.

my lungs are flooded
with all the words i never said to you--
i never said i needed you to keep me afloat.

and now i am drowning
because of my own stupidity--
my mother always warned me of this.

the weight of us is so heavy,
but only to me--
for you, it does not exist.

because to you,
i am nothing--
just a girl at the bottom of the ocean.

-c.h.

he used to love me, i think

he wasn't someone i saw coming, but they never are, are they? he was the most beautiful mistake i ever made, if you consider it a mistake. but i never thought it was. merely the wrong place and wrong time. people would roll their eyes and shake their heads, but we never asked for their approval. to us, it was all right. every last moment. he was a compilation of all the beautiful things in the world that had strings attached. he was a summer thunderstorm with the fallen tree that blocks your driveway. he was the stars in the sky that died centuries ago. he was the high and the low, the beautiful fire and it's scorching burn. i wrote poetry about him for months after he was gone and with every word a wound reopened but the pain reminds me of him so i keep writing. i can't stop. won't stop. i used to not be able to write, but now i can't stop and it hurts so much. he hurts so much, but he is so beautiful. i will never be able to say he is not beautiful, and that is the most sad thing of all. he stopped calling me beautiful a long time ago, the words left his mind, slipped off his tongue in another conversation with someone who means more than me now. the most painful thing about love is that somebody has to stop eventually and it's never going to be you. it will always be them. they will be empty before you're even at halfway and you'll be left with gallons of love and nowhere to put them. the obvious thing to do would be to love yourself, but your eyesight is clouded with agony, so you can't see what's two feet in front of you anymore. so instead it drips out, useless, wasted on meaningless kisses in the middle of the night behind your neighbor's garage, pointless promises and grasping hands under sheets that aren't clean, metaphorically or literally. i still write about him, even now. it's been months since he told me he didn't love me anymore and i still write about him as if he does. i used to not be able to write but now i can't stop and he is so beautiful, and even now that's all i see and that is the most sad thing of all.

-c.h.

31

the phone
at one point, he'd say, "i love you," into the phone,
and i would smile.
now, the line is dead. the phone doesn't ring.
now, he says nothing.

i say, "please come back," into the static.
the phone beeps, and then there is the deadly silence.
a dark reminder.

i cry.

                -c.h.

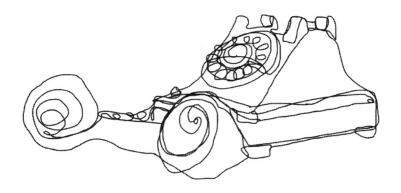

i think you might have ruined me (and you don't even know it)
ever since the beginning, i knew i'd do anything for you. i knew i
would do anything to see you smile; your smile was so beautiful. i
knew i would break my own bones trying to please you, hammer
nails into my heart, peel away the cracked pieces and dump them,
bloody, into your hands even if you didn't ask for them (the fact that
you'd hold them for a moment was a privilege in and of itself). it was
a drunk obsession, i stumbled after you like i was a lost dog hoping
that someone, someone would just take me home, i swayed under
your gaze even if you never let it rest on me for long. i clung to every
part of you, all the parts you never gave me, all the parts i knew i
could have loved–the parts i did love even though you never asked
me to. you were the source of all my pain and yet i wanted you to
end it all. i longed for you to take away the pain, you were the
bandaid and the bullet, the gun at the soldier's head who was fatally
shot seconds before. the one thing that kills me is the one thing that
saves me; and it's you, you, you. it's always been you.

-c.h.

and he looks at her so delicately, with such a twinkle in his eyes, that i cannot help but let out a soft, "oh," from between my lips.

"hmm?" he doesn't take his eyes off of the girl asleep on his lap, her dark hair falling across her shoulders and face, and her hand resting gently on his.

"you're in love with her, aren't you?"

he smiles, and tears his gaze from her to meet mine. "of course i am, and you aren't?" there isn't a trace of sarcasm or lightness in his voice; he is completely serious– '*and you aren't*'?

"well, no, but i suppose i can see why you are," i reply, and he chuckles dryly.

"you suppose you can see why…" he murmurs, more to himself than anything, and lowers his eyes so that he can once again stare adoringly at the sleeping girl.

"she is beautiful," i say, in an effort to redeem myself, "and she's very kind, and intelligent."

"oh, i know," he cuts me off, "but she's so much more." he smiles and twines a strand of her hair around his fingers. "she's someone that you never know you need, until you meet her. and she's someone you never know you won't be able to live without, until you lose her."

"does she love you, too?" i have to know, i realize. surely, she loves him back. she must.

"in her own little way, she does." he frowns. they have problems when it comes to this; it's obvious. "but i know she's loved others, too." his eyes darken. "loves others, i mean."

"she does love him, and i'm sure it hurts you."

he knows who i'm talking about when i say 'him.' he sighs, and shrugs. "it does, but only a little bit. he won't have her in the end."

it's an awfully arrogant thing to say, i think; *'he won't have her in the end'*. he's so sure she'll be his. "i don't understand. how can you be so sure?"

"you never saw us together," he says simply, as if it were obvious, "not when we were really together. if you did, you would understand." his eyes cloud as he remembers. "oh, us, together… together, we could take over the world."

-c.h.

things i see as god

observation #1: the boy with the black pea coat sits in the back of the class and scribbles in his notebook. he doesn't answer questions. he always looks down, except when he looks over at the girl one row over and two desks up.

observation #2: the subject of these glances does not seem to know she is just that. she is attentive and focused and does not spend any time looking one row over and two desks back at the boy with the black pea coat. she would have no reason to.

observation #3: there is a couple, and they seem like the spitting image of a dream high school love: she wears his jacket and he walks her to class holding her hand. his jacket collar is high enough that people don't notice the bruises.

observation #4: the boy in the black pea coat is in love with the girl one row over and two desks up. he stares too much.

observation #5: the girl does not know that she is loved like she is, at least by him. why should she? he never talks.

observation #6: some bruises are too dark to be covered up with concealer. people are starting to notice.

observation #7: a student keeps a bottle of adderall in her backpack. the prescription is hers, but it's not for her. it's almost finals, her friends say. they can't study without it. she knows it's wrong, but she could use the money.

observation #8: the couple enters the room, except they are separate. she doesn't have his jacket and he doesn't hold her hand. she moves away from him, next to the boy with the black pea coat. he checks the bruises every time she sits down. after a week, they've faded.

observation #9: the boy with the black pea coat won't stop

staring at the girl one row over, two desks up. one day, she turns around and catches his eye. she smiles. there is hope.

observation #10: the girl with the backpack sells adderall to the boy who beat his girlfriend. he tries to flirt with her, and she tells him to fuck off. he hits the wall as he walks away. she wonders how the girl didn't see it coming.

observation #11: the girl looks back at the boy with the black pea coat more often. he has pretty eyes. she can see the blue in them from here.

observation #12: sometimes she must talk to her ex boyfriend and the places he hit her burn. the boy with the black pea coat is always there. he says nothing, just watches, and makes eye contact with her when he leaves. silence is the loudest thing at times.

observation #13: the boy with the black pea coat does not love the girl one row over and two desks up anymore. which is sad, because she was just starting to love him.

observation #14: the girl with the backpack uses the money from selling adderall to buy christmas presents for her family. two days later she is caught with it in her backpack and is suspended for three days. no medication on campus, they said. she thinks about the toy she got her little brother.

observation #15: on christmas day, the girl with the backpack helps her little brother open a new lego set. the boy with the black pea coat starts looking up more and the girl one row over and two desks back stops looking back. she never gets to tell him he has pretty eyes. the girl next to him does it for her. there is kissing instead of hitting. but what once was lingers. it always lingers.

-c.h.

eulogy of a broken heart
everything falls apart
everything dies
your hands crumbled to dust
and fell through my fingertips
i lost you oh god
i lost you

i thought that
you would stay
but you blew away with
the wind and faded from
my eyes i wonder
where you are now

you used to
tell me i was
something otherworldly and
i told you the same
but you went on an adventure
and never came back

they say that
graveyards are the
scariest of places but
for me it is the mirror
because when i look into it
you are not by my side anymore

and nothing
is scarier
than that

                              -c.h.

metaphorically speaking

it's impossible to describe exactly how you made me feel but you were like a cold drink on an eighty degree day, you were like freshly shaven legs, you were like feeling the beach sand in between your toes and the waves lapping against your shins, you were refreshing, renewing. i don't know how to describe exactly how it felt when you touched me but it was like a hot towel pressed against my skin, it was like the slightest of electrocutions, it was like feeling the warm sun beat down on your back, it was intense, warm. i could never explain exactly how it felt when you broke me but it felt like stubbing your foot on the corner of the table a dozen times over, it was like having a cough and not being able to swallow your breath, it was like chopping vegetables and cutting your finger, it was sudden, painful. i don't know to describe any of this properly but i guess i'm doing the best i can given the fact that when you left you took all of me with you.

-c.h.

succubus
i'm still waiting
for the bite marks
to heal.

       -c.h.

schoolgirl's lament
i want to kiss you
but you like the hard girls
with rough teeth
and dry hands
the wet girls
with slick tongues
and untied laces

the girls who
suck the life out of you
like they shotgun cigarette
smoke into your naked chest

i know your fingers
make a mess of her body
i know your eyes gloss
and your mouth gapes
as she makes a mess
out of you

she's beautiful
in a chaotic way
i will never understand

i look at my buttoned blouse
and toothpaste teeth
and i know
i am beautiful to some
but it's just a shame
i'm not beautiful
to you

                                        -c.h.

i wrote this the day before you left me (i wonder how i knew)
enough is enough
is enough
and i told you
we couldn't
but you always said
we can

you've always been
a believer
in fate and us
but now
we've reached the end
of everything

you told me
that you
loved every part of
my broken
soul and that night
i cried

enough is enough
is enough
we were wrong to
think otherwise
because time will always
run out

-c.h.

the poem that got me death threats
she let him touch her;
she's a whore!
but why is it your business,
what she does behind closed doors?

she showed some skin,
such a slut!
it's simply a shoulder,
that doesn't spark lust.

her breasts are covered,
barely even exposed,
but you all shame her
like she's wearing no clothes.

slut, whore, and skank,
all unnecessary titles,
used so frequently,
we don't see them as vile.

if a girl is unpure and dirty
because of what she did in bed,
maybe you should backtrack
and start looking at his hands instead.

-c.h.

43

in rewind
after you left,
i was told
to try to replay us
backwards
because then it's not
falling apart,
it's coming together.

i think that
us in rewind
is still just as
painful
because it begins
with you rebuilding me,
and us being happy
for a while,
until one day
you just forget about me.

but then again,
isn't that how it happened,
anyway?

-c.h.

the saddest thing
in the weeks after,
i traced my fingers along
the cracks in the porcelain
in my heart and i could
still feel the imprint
where your hands
used to rest.

there are chips missing,
exposing the bleeding red
beneath, and i know
that those pieces
rest in your pocket.

of course,
you had to leave
with some sort of
piece of me.

i'm not angry
that you took
a part of my heart.

i'm just sad,
because even though
you have it,
it won't make us
any less of strangers.

-c.h.

some people will say this is a prostitute (others will be
reminded of themselves)

the girl on the corner
of Main Street waits
for someone to say
they need her again

she has golden hair
and dull green eyes
but she is beautiful
even though she is
horribly broken

she spends her nights
at bars with her
brittle hands quaking for
something more than gray
cigarette smoke and dirty
sheets with dirty men
in them

she aches for you
and hopes you will come
back soon but alas
you have been gone
for so long and
gone you shall continue
to be.

                    -c.h.

i guess this means i'm moving on
you were here
and then suddenly
you were gone
in the blink of an eye

i still miss you
even though i can no longer
recall the color of your eyes
or the texture of your hands

all i know is that
you loved me
but you never loved me
enough

we were together
but i've gone
and forgotten
the rest.

-c.h.

galactic

you called me a galaxy.
you played connect the dots with
the freckles on my arms
and called them constellations.
you told me i had stars in my eyes
and celestial matter in my veins.
you said falling for me was like
falling into a black hole;
endless, exhilarating.

but your words struck me like meteors,
and your glare burned me like the sun.
it occurred to me that, like the moon,
you were only with me at night,
and i never saw all of who you were.

we ended like a supernova,
in an explosion that was slow and fast
at the same time.

-c.h.

boys i've loved and the end of the world #2

"they say it's a solar flare, the biggest one they've ever seen," he says with a sigh.

"are you scared?" i ask.

he runs his hand through his hair. "i don't think so. it's inevitable, right?"

"sure. but aren't you scared of death?"

"why would i be? sometimes i try to get there early." there is a smile on his face, but the weight of his words is still so heavy in the air.

"you never take anything seriously," i mumble, more to myself than anything, but he hears me.

"sure i do. i took you seriously."

"but you left."

"still. you were my favorite thing," he says, quietly, as if he is afraid of what i'll do when i hear it.

"then why did you push me away? after all that time, all those memories, and you just… told me to leave."

"i was made up of a million mistakes already. i didn't want you to become another one."

"but i did anyway, didn't i?" i press.

"not exactly. because i let you go, you met him, and you were happy. and even though it wasn't with me, it was… it was something, you know? something to feel good about."

"so in a way, it was always about me, wasn't it?"

he looks at me then, and his blue eyes are sad, like they always are.

"until the end," he says.

-c.h

a poem on how i realized i still love you
there was something about the way
you told me you loved me that sounded like a song,
and it's sad that i never got a chance to memorize it,
for the melody reminded me of my childhood.

you were so gentle in the way you treated me
that it's no wonder you were so gentle in leaving, too.
i guess you really did mean it
when you said you'd never try and hurt me.

i think i'm going to miss you for a very long time.
and i know i'll be okay,
but i just wish i could be okay
with you.

-c.h.

the truth

they say that all love stories end in tragedy. no happy ending lasts forever. in the end, there is only one way out, and you must go it alone. but i thought, for some reason, that you wouldn't leave until you had to. i thought when you said you weren't leaving, you meant it; that you'd keep your promise as long as you could. i thought that you would stay.

the saddest part is that i know you, and i know what to expect from you when you're broken. i know that when they ask you about me, you'll tell them i was too opposite of you, that my smile held too many secrets and had tasted too many lips. you'll tell them my heart was like ice but my words were like fire, and they burned your skin. you'll tell them i laughed enough for 1,000 drunken men but that i was always laughing at someone else. you'll tell them i'm cold. hard. you'll tell them i left, and you'll say you were glad.

but you won't tell them how you told me you loved me through tears late at night. you won't tell them that i pulled the stitches from my lips so i could bleed my story into your hands. you won't tell them i wrote you letters, essays on my soul. you won't tell them that you kissed me like i was water and you hadn't drunk in days. you won't tell them i never wanted to leave, you won't say that you were the one who told me it was over. you won't tell them how my heart was ice, but it melted for you.

when they ask me about you, i will tell them that we said we were in love, and i will tell them you lied.

they don't need to know anything else.

-c.h.

here's the reason why i left you
we are a fire;
we are flaming
with red-hot passion
and we burn
and burn
and burn

we are a fire;
it only took a spark
for us to light a wildfire
and we burn
and burn
and burn

we are a fire;
we need oxygen to live
but we are too close to breathe
and we burn
and burn
and burn
out.

-c.h.

a princess poem
cinderella, cinderella,
she lived her life in shame.
it wasn't until a man saved her
that she finally tasted fame.

"rapunzel, rapunzel,
just let down your hair!"
Prince Charming is upset,
he actually needs her help, how unfair!

belle, belle,
would have been content with her books,
but she had to be kidnapped
to change a man's looks.

aurora, aurora,
what kind of curse is this?
that the only cure is the touch
of an unknown man's lips?

snow white, snow white,
what a housewife you are.
you're much more than cleaning,
this role is so subpar.

princesses, princesses,
what a repetitive story.
all about needing a man
to achieve glory.

women, women,
you're not alone.
no longer do you need a king;
you can be a queen on your own.

-c.h.

i swear one day i'll be able to smile by myself again
it's hard; not seeing him anymore. i try to remember everything i can, but it's never enough. i can feel the smallest of details, the little things, fading away. i'm reaching, grasping at silver strands of memories as they float away. i want them to come back; i never want to forget him, but he is so far away and he cannot kiss me from where he is. he can't kiss anybody from where he is. the last time i saw him, he looked tired but he smiled anyways; he touched his fingers to my mouth and told me to try my hardest to smile, too. i smiled only because he told me to, only because he made me happy enough for it to not feel stitched on with needles. he was stargazing and fingertips brushing in movies and a time bomb. he was ice cream and a fuse that was lit from the very first day. we were always counting down, there was a clock inside of us and we were just counting down the days. even when it reached zero we never believed that time had actually run out. when i got the phone call, i hung up as soon as i heard the doctor tell me, "i'm sorry," and i grabbed the photos of us on my bedroom wall and held them tight to my chest. pictures don't do him justice, but they are all i have except my tired mind. my mind is always running to find him; i am always trying to find him out there, somewhere. is he happy now? i pray that he is, i pray to a god i don't believe in that if he does one thing for me, it is that he is happy, now. on the worst of days i remember how it felt to kiss him and how he told me to smile. he told me it was okay and even though it never was and never will be, i smile because he told me to.

-c.h.

an excerpt (#2)
"did he break your heart?"

"no, i don't think so," she answers, but she sounds uncertain. the question has made her reconsider. after a moment, she says, "he hurt me. there's no use in denying that."

he looks at her. "how badly?"

she shrugs, looks down at her shoes. "enough to make me cry. enough... just enough. he hurt me enough."

he blinks, and rolls a lighter between his fingers. he's not a smoker, but she is, and he thought he would give it to her, maybe. just to try and get through to her. "did you love him?"

she laughs at this, and tucks her knees into her chest, "nah, not even close." she sighs, "i could have though, i think." her eyes darken, "if he'd given me the chance to."

he's unsure of how to respond, so he hands her the lighter. "it's for you," he mumbles, and she smiles for a fleeting second, takes it from his grasp, and then hands it back.

"no thanks," she says, and then explains, "i'm trying to quit. i wanna go somewhere, live a long time. can't do that if i smoke, ya know?"

"yeah, i know, i just thought–"

she squeezes his hand, "i know what you thought, and it's sweet. you're sweet." he smiles, and for a moment, she smiles back at him. then it slides off her face, and he waits for her to speak.

"it just, it just sucks getting fucked over, ya know?" she runs a hand through her hair, "like, he was so important. it wasn't that i wanted to date him or any of that, but he was just important. he used to say that i was important too, and that's what hurts the most, i think. the fact that he just randomly decided that i wasn't anymore."

he opens his mouth, but she keeps going.

"so i guess, in a way, he might have broken my heart. not enough for me to feel it for a long time, but just enough to remind me that he meant something to me and he fucking walked away."

"he hurt you enough," he echoes her previous words.

"yeah, yeah," she wipes a tear away with the palm of her hand, "he hurt me enough."

-c.h.

losing you

time is everything and we are running out of it--*tick tick tick*--my eyes twitch and my hands tremble but shaking doesn't bring you back--*won't bring you back*--shaking only rattles our bones and cracks our fingers--*crack crack crack*--and i cry for you--*please please please stay stay stay* with me--but you can't--*you can't--we* can't anymore--time is everything and we are running out of it--*tick tick*--slipping through our fingers like sand and blowing away with the wind--*gone gone gone--you are gone gone gone* and i reach in the dark for you but i can't see your eyes any more *where are you--* you *promised--lies lies lies*--time is everything and we are running out of it--*tick*

-c.h.

an abstract look on my high school years
FRESHMAN: bitten nails. scratchy scalp. boys are nothing. i still miss him. six months. boys have to be nothing. forgotten homework. told the teacher i don't understand. refused tutoring. can't seem to write anymore. i saw him today. he kissed me. i believed his apology. second chances. second chances. he lied again. i'm still hurting. now i can write. boys are nothing. boys are nothing.

SOPHOMORE. new boy. new love. want to say new me. still the same. he's too much. i don't deserve him. he leaves. tells everyone he hates me. boys are too much. music. invest in the music. he smiles at me. he's somebody i deserve. shaky fingers. swollen lips. i kiss him too much. i get bored. i leave. boys are nothing.

JUNIOR: call him on the phone. i say i miss him. he says it back. he curls his fingers into her. he's a liar. filthy liar. i give up everything to love him. he only wants me to boost his ego. says i look real pretty all fucked up that. i still think about his tongue. still blame myself for everything. i know i didn't deserve that pain. but i accept anyway. told him i tried to give him what he wanted. in the end he's the one left crying. i don't understand it even now. boys are nothing.

SENIOR: he kisses me. i smile. think of his teeth. time is a bomb. don't know what will happen. love him too much to stop. he treats me better than i deserve. i take it. take him. i can't imagine him in love with someone else. i am his. some people call this poison. i call it the antidote. i told myself boys are nothing. but they aren't. they aren't nothing. they aren't everything. they just are. he holds my hand. i fold into him. boys are.

-c.h.

59

a misconstrued metaphor

people say that the way you know
how loved a book is
is by how worn the pages are.
how creased the spine is.
how wrinkled the corners are
from bending them.

i want to think that
you took this idea
to heart when it came
to how you treated me.
maybe you thought
the more broken and bent
i was the more loved i would look.

but i am not a book.
you cannot pick me up
just to put me down again.
i am not something to be skimmed.
read all of me, or don't read any at all.

i'm not demanding
you take forever
to finish me.
i won't even mind
if you don't enjoy me.

i'm just asking that
you treat me with care,
and walk away having learned
something new.

                                    -c.h.

ivory
i wonder if they notice

how i touch piano keys
like they can breathe

-c.h.

a twelve-word story
"so, what do you think about me?"
"well," he said, "i don't."

-c.h.

on the refugee crisis

(follow the punctuation)

silence their cries.
we can not

let the world know
about their struggles, we must
keep quiet.
we can not
expose ourselves.
it is the just thing, to
do, and we are strong.
we know it is a frightening thing to
always live in fear.
but we are tired of how they

complain.
we have no reason to
give them what they need.
we have to
tape over their mouths.
we can't
speak the truth.
they
are not innocent.
we must know we

have loud voices.
they do not.
they should believe
there is no reason that
they are important.

-c.h.

(read from bottom to top)

honest texts to my ex i'm too scared to send

you can't keep resurfacing like a rotted fish in the ocean on a hot day. it makes me sick, every time.

i don't care if you dreamt about me. please don't let me know that i still haunt you at night. it'll make me think there's still something here.

sometimes i'm afraid i might still be in love with you. out of everything, that's what i'm most scared of.

i want you to know that i miss the way you made me laugh. can we have that again someday?

you still make me cry, you fuck

you always tell me you're still not okay but what about me? what makes you think i'm okay? i had my heart broken too remember?

nothing felt as easy at the beginning as you did. but nothing was as impossible in the end as you were.

i'm sorry. i've always been sorry.

i don't think i'm ever going to love somebody like i loved you, but i'm okay with that. i don't want to feel this type of pain ever again.

one day, you're going to look back on me and smile. you'll have to.

we can't dwell on this forever.

-c.h.

write about something other than love

that is what they tell me
they say
to write about something
more challenging than love

like coming to terms
with your abusive relationship

isn't challenging

like learning to stop
loving someone who
once gave you everything

isn't a battle

like figuring out
how to use art as
a catharsis instead of
not sleeping
not eating
not breathing

isn't a hard thing to do

so this is me saying
i will write about whatever
makes me scream
makes me cry
makes me laugh
makes me smile

and if that's
love
or a lack thereof
then so be it

i didn't bleed
just so you could say
my blood isn't

red enough
for you

-c.h.

you are not the one bleeding here
you call it free speech
and you hit the gas pedal--
drive until you can't,
and it's not the people
that stop you.

i look down at the bodies
and i wonder if you'll ever recognize
the blood on your hands as being anything
but your own.

(especially when it's not.)

                              -c.h.

this is why we can't stay away from each other

you said hello
and you meant it--
i could hear it in your voice

that you wanted to know me
to see me
to feel me

you said goodbye
and you were lying--
i could hear it in your voice

that you didn't want to leave me
to forget me
to free me

i want to say
i meant the goodbye
as much as i did the hello

but i know i didn't
i know
i can't

-c.h.

maybe a love story will catch your attention
i fell in love with a muslim boy once.
he kissed flower petals into my shoulder blades
and traced arabic with his tongue onto my stomach.

his love was one of the most beautiful things i had
ever experienced.

he told me one night how scared he was.
how he was afraid to walk down the street sometimes.
how, even though he didn't wear a hijab, his sister did,
and after an attack, he always tried to convince her
to take it off.

sometimes, he would cry.
heavy, broken sobs into my chest.
he told me once that he hated who he was,
and i told him that is what they wanted him to do.

i know he hides his quran when his non-muslim friends
come over.
i know he feels like he has to justify everything he does.
i know there are times where he feels as though he is trapped.

we fell apart months ago.
he couldn't love both himself
and me.
and as much as i wanted to,
i could not teach him what pride is
when for so long, the world
has told him he is undeserving of it.

                                        -c.h.

69

i can't tell if we're still in love (i hope we are)
and there are times
when i am sad
that i think of you,
and i become sadder,
just in a happier kind of way.

i remember when i kissed you
and you told me you froze
because you thought i never would,
and i still smile knowing
that i'd planned to all along.

you told me you loved me
and i still feel the shiver
running down my spine.
you were so beautiful to me.
you've never stopped in my eyes.

and there are times
when i am sad
that i think of you,
and how i said i love you too
because darling, i did

and darling, i still do.

-c.h.

as a woman
i wrote once in a poem
that woman are hostages
of expectation.

it has been almost three years
since those words left
my mind and bled onto paper

and i have yet to find
them false.

society is full of contradictions
and it is built this way so we
are always stuck on the ground.
we do one thing we think they want
but then they tell us they want another,
and it goes in a cycle. we can never
climb over the ledge.

they tell us to wear makeup,
so we dab foundation onto
our skin and brush on silky
highlighters and mascara,
only for them to tell us
it's too much-- they like it
natural.

so we wipe off the makeup,
walk out onto the streets
with a face that has undereye bags,
splotches of acne, uneven skin,
and then they tell us that
we look sloppy-- we should try
harder.

we are taught through the media

that women are sexual creatures.
everywhere we go, we see the pictures
and hear the songs.

if we refuse to be sexual, we are ridiculed.
if we harness it for ourselves, we are crucified.
if we don't put out, we are hated.
if we do and are proud, we are hated even more.

men want to see us naked and submissive,
naked and insecure
naked and silent,
not naked and dominant,
naked and confident,
naked and loud.

when a woman posts
a halfnaked photo
because she wants to,
she will be ridiculed by the same
men who watch lesbian porn
in between harassing women
online for taking control of
the sexuality they demanded
we have.

they tell us to love ourselves
but then they bash us for it
if we aren't what they want,
if loving ourselves means going against
everything they've told us.

so women find themselves trapped--
trapped because every move
is a wrong one.

"wear makeup,
but not because you want to."

"be sexual,
but don't be proud of it."

"love yourself,
but not too much.

you may get away from us then."

-c.h.

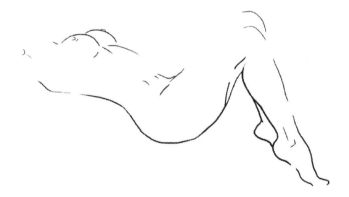

i didn't know you'd regret me that much
your eyes are full of anger,
your sneer is full of hate.

you never seemed to understand
you have to watch the steps you take.

your methods of forgetting
are far less than futile

you know you can't erase
how you felt when you saw me smile.

so call me what you please,
say i was a mistake

but you can't always reverse
what you thought was fate.

                            -c.h.

tidal

she is the moon and i am the beach;
she is strong and i am weak.
you are the ocean, stuck between,
and she keeps pulling you away from me.

she is always there, tugging you back,
but she shows herself at night, when the sky is black.
her skin is pale, her eyes are bright,
it's the reason i ask: why even put up a fight?

you come to me in the morning,
and hold me tight at noon,
but when the evening comes you leave again,
just like you always do.

she is the moon and i am the beach,
she is strong and i am weak.
though she always gives you back to me,
it just hurts more each time you leave.

you are the beautiful ocean,
trapped in this game of tug o' war,
but soon i'll be eroded,
and have nothing left to give you (or her) anymore.

-c.h.

what ruined us (or maybe you just didn't care)
i loved you
vibrantly. entirely.
constantly.
like there was nothing
else in the world
worth loving.
like you were the end.

i loved you
angrily. maddeningly.
yearningly.
like the distance
was the only problem.
like it was the only reason
you weren't always there.

i loved you
sadly. delicately.
wishfully.
like you were breaking me
but i still wouldn't blame you.
like your promises were real
and you actually believed in them.

you loved me
casually. easily.
partially.
like i didn't mean as much
as you said i did.
like you didn't love me
at all.

-c.h.

the boys i've loved and the end of the world #3
"do you think it'll be quick or slow?" i ask him. we are sitting on a bench, separate sides, but it is comfortable.

"i'm not sure. do you think it'll hurt?" he responds, looking at me with eyes that have never been anything but kind.

"i'm sorry if i ever hurt you," i blurt out, because i feel like i need to say it.

"you didn't break my heart," he says honestly, "we fell apart in a way that didn't let you."

"i wouldn't have even if i'd had the chance." there is a pause, and the trees cast shadows over us. "you taught me how to love myself, i hope you know that."

he smiles. "i didn't teach you anything. you learned how to on your own."

"it was because of you, though." i pause, then ask, "do you tell her that you love her every chance you get?"

"of course." he fumbles with his hands. "there's only so many chances left to say it, anyways."

we sit together, and i tuck my knees into my chest and rest my chin on them. he watches the sky, frowning, and i want to say that he is too good to be wiped out by a solar flare, but i don't. instead i say, "i'm so fucking scared."

he reaches over and rests his hand on my shoulder. "me too." "i learned from you that love doesn't always have to end nasty. sometimes, it just stops."

he nods, agreeing, and squeezes my shoulder once.

"maybe that'll be how the world ends," he suggests, "it won't end terribly. it'll just stop."

-c.h.

so this is how it feels to have someone give up on you
i remember when you first
told me you loved me,
and you held my hands in yours and
whispered it again and again
in my ear until i was in tears,
and my heart was flying out of my chest.

there is so much time and space
between us now and i do not know
how to make it go away.
i do not like the distance in the slightest
but i can not figure out how
to make it disappear. i don't think
you ever wanted to leave, really.
but you have always been impatient.

i spend my time counting out
the minutes and seconds and days
and hours that have passed since
you've gone.
i know you are with her;
it hurts me so, but i cannot forget it,
no matter how hard i try.
it's funny how the most painful memories
are the ones that stay.

she is not a poet like i am.
she cannot make you sound beautiful
the way i do, she cannot write you
love poems that can be framed
and put on the wall.
i hope she doesn't love you as well as i did,
as well as i do, so maybe you will realize, me.
after all this time.

one time, you told me you wanted

to marry me. i think you still do,
deep down. i hope she hears it when
you say my name. "i don't love her, anymore,"
you tell her, but all she hears is,
"i do, i do."

-c.h.

cherry blossom kisses

age seven: when you can finally understand what the preacher is saying, you start telling your parents to read you part of the bible every night. it was almost as though the stories they told were bedtime stories, fiction, but your parents read them with such conviction and your preacher cried out to God with such trust and devotion that you decide there's no way so many people live their lives through a fairytale. you find church boring, so your parents sign you up for Sunday school and you spend it playing with cars and talking about fairness with a mahogany-haired boy your age.

age eight: your friend is in your third grade class and you sit on the swings at recess. he tells you he doesn't understand any of the bible. you confess that you don't understand it either, but all of the adults do, so one day the two of you will understand its meaning too. he says his older brother has been hanging out with a boy a lot recently. "just like us," you point out, but he shakes his head. "no," he whispers, "like they go in his bedroom and shut the door. there's no sounds or anything. i don't even think they play video games."

age nine: one day he shows up crying at Sunday school. "they found him... kissing the other boy," he sobs and your mouth gapes, horrified. he presses himself into you and you hug him like a good friend would. "dad hit him and mommy cried." you ask your parents if you can take him home for the afternoon. you planned on taking his mind off of it, but you end up sitting in your bedroom with the door shut, not even playing video games.

age ten: he spends most of his time at your house. whenever he can escape his parents he appears at your door. his brother hasn't been around for a year or so. sometimes he'll cry into your shoulder and your heart hurts for him.

age eleven: you have your first Valentine: a girl your age, with hair as golden as the sun and eyes as green as the leaves in summer. she hands you the heart-shaped card after school, her cheeks red from both the chilly air and nerves. you say yes, but no heat rises to your cheeks. you smile and she reaches out and holds your hand. your fingertips are numb by the time you let go as she steps onto her bus, but you assume it's because the cold.

age twelve: you have your first kiss, with your first Valentine. it's at his birthday party. she pulls you away from him as he blows out the candles and tugs you behind a tree. "i like you a lot," she murmure shyly. she goes up on her tiptoes and presses her lips against yours. "fireworks, he kept saying it felt like fireworks," he'd said about his brother. her lips held no spark.

age thirteen: you don't talk to that girl anymore, the girl who kissed you at his birthday party last year. she moved last winter, but for some reason it didn't bother you. you stay glued to his side, or rather he stays glued to yours, but either way you like the way things are. you join the church choir for the hell of it, but as you sing about God's love you find your voice falling flat.

age fourteen: you enter high school, nervous but reassured with him next to you. you smile broadly when you're with him; he's your best friend, the only friend you'd ever need. on the five year anniversary of the night his parents caught his brother, he shows up at your door and cries because his brother still hasn't called and his parents don't care anymore. "'monster,' they call him, 'abomination.' but he isn't that. he's just a human," he whispers, and you wonder when he got so mature.

age fifteen: you go to your first big party and one of the older kids talks you into drinking. you end up drunk and stumble through the crowd, trying to find him. when you do, he's sitting on the curb with his head in his hands. you mumble something incomprehensible and sit next to him. "do you think you'll remember anything about tonight, tomorrow?" he asks, and you shake your head, laughing. "so you won't remember this." he kisses you under the street lamp. sparks. you remembered nothing but that the next morning.

age sixteen: you never ask him about that party. and he never brings it up, until one night his brother shows up at his house with the same boy he'd been caught with holding his hand. they have gotten married, and are about to finish college. they've applied to adopt a baby. they are happy, successful. his parents take one look at their intertwined fingers and slam the door in their faces. soon after, he shows up at your door, and you pull him into your room. "i'm afraid," he admits through tears, "i'm afraid i'm going to end up just like my brother; shunned and hated by my family." you tell him no, grab his shoulders and tell him that isn't possible. "yes it is," he whispers, "last year, at the party..." "i know," you say, and he blinks before he kisses you again.

age seventeen: you secretly hold hands in church, underneath your suit jackets. his hand sends electricity up your arm and through your body, and you stare down the preacher as he shouts about sin and love and hell. after the service, he takes you to the cemetery out back and kisses you furiously behind a tree. "i love you," he says, "i need you." you kiss him hard in response, but then you feel a hand that isn't his clamp down on your shoulder. you jolt away from him and find your father glaring at you, furious and hateful. he glances at your intertwined fingers and yanks you away from him. "i will not have a faggot in my family," he snarls, "why am i not surprised you're one too?" your father sneers at him, "you already have one ungodly creature in your family." you're being pulled away from him, your father's grip is tight on your wrist, you say, "i love you," and your father slaps you. he drags you home and hits you again and again while your mother cries and begs for him to stop, but he keeps hitting you...

age eighteen: it's been one year since your father beat you to death in your kitchen. he still visits you every week, lays a new bouquet on your grave. always cherry blossoms; from the tree he last kissed you under. your mother stops by sometimes, more out of obligation and public reputation than grief. your father can't visit you from a jail cell, nor would he want to. sometimes when he comes to your grave, he brings the bible you'd had when you were a kid, and stares at its faded cover. one day, he rips the pages to shreds, each one of them, tears streaking his cheeks. "we just fell in love," he cries, "we just did what God told us to do."

-c.h.

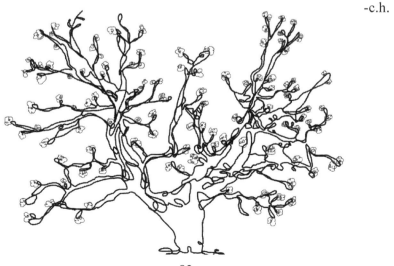

83

i will always find you too beautiful to bear
i have spent hours
flipping through poetry books
trying to find something
that portrays just how
lovely he is to me,
but i haven't found
a single stanza that
explains it well enough.

i do not think he has eyes
as blue as the ocean
or hair as golden as the sun;
cliché metaphors don't
do him justice.

he is not a sentence that's been
written a million times by
a million different people
who have never met him--

why should it be used to describe him
when they don't know who they're describing?

when you step outside
on the first day of spring,
everything is green,
the sky is blue,
and you can smell
the beauty in the air--

that is him,
fresh and bright and beautiful.
i want to tell him this,
tell him just how beautiful
he is to me,
but i can't.

you see,
he is so beautiful,
but he isn't mine.

-c.h.

writer's block
and i wish i could write
about you,
because i want to tell
the world
how beautiful you are
to me.

but i can't,
and as you press
your lips into my
collarbone,
i think,

maybe this is a good thing.
maybe this is just
for us.

                              -c.h.

eyes

you know how they say the eyes are the windows to the soul? that's how it is when i meet your gaze from across the room. when i find you, and blue meets brown and everything freezes. and for a moment, just a single moment, the world shifts around us.

everything we were flashes past. for an instant, i can feel how it felt to be loved by you again; a feeling i thought i didn't know anymore. but then, i am transported back to the present, and i am stuck now with what we have become: a shattered, empty shell of what once was the strongest love i'd ever known. and it saddens me, not because i still love you, but because i know that if we had worked a little harder, i still would. i know that if i had spoken up sooner instead of burying it all inside of me, i would still be completely tied up in you.

i let you get away with things i normally would have never stood for. i let you kiss other girls because distance was hard and we needed that release. i let you stop talking to me for days because i knew you had a busy schedule. i made excuse, after excuse, after excuse for you, because i didn't want to see the truth. eventually, i had to raise my head and meet its burning gaze. and by then, it was too late.

when we lock eyes from across the room, i can hear everything you want to say. i can see the pain and the anger and the sadness and i know you can see it in my eyes too.

eyes are the windows to the soul. my soul says, "i'm sorry we never got a real chance." your soul whispers back, "i'm sorry i made you think i didn't want one."

-c.h.

in short
the way you dipped
your fingers into me
left me widemouthed
and empty.

you took everything.

-c.h.

"tell me, why do we romanticize pain?" he asks, staring not at her, but up at the clouds.

"i think we do it to understand it better," she answers, and he frowns.

"how does that work? there's nothing beautiful about pain. beautiful things can come out of pain, sure, but pain in and of itself is not beautiful."

"maybe... maybe, we do it because it's the only way we can stand to think about it. we, as humans, we want to reject the ugly things in life. take 'ugly' with a grain of salt, though, because in the past, those we have rejected for being 'ugly' weren't ugly at all. but our brains are limited, and easily corrupted by preconceived ideas. so maybe, because we can't get rid of pain, we try and make it more glamorous, so we won't just shut it away. because part of coping with pain in a healthy way is being open about it."

he laughs, and looks at her. "you're very smart, you know that?" she feels herself blushing. "i guess."

he touches her hand, briefly. "it doesn't make it right, does it?" he inquires, "it's not good to make pain seem beautiful. it makes people think being in pain is good, that it makes you beautiful. so really, by trying to understand it better, we really aren't understanding it at all."

"well, nobody wants to be sad, but everyone wants to be beautiful, whatever their definition of 'beautiful' may be. so if you're sad, romanticizing it may be the only way to feel beautiful."

"but it's toxic. it hurts you. if you become so convinced that your pain is beautiful, that it's art, then you never want to be happy."

"i wouldn't say that," she squints her eyes, pursing her lips, "everyone wants to be happy. but i think... i think people just settle, after awhile. they get tired. so they rest assured knowing that people on social media find their sadness attractive and romantic, so they still feel beautiful, in a sense."

"is that what you think?"

"yeah, it is," she says, "maybe i'm wrong, though. i don't know. i've just never really understood why people think kissing scars is going to make them go away. or that saying suicide is beautiful is going to make it stop."

"because everyone wants to be beautiful, right?" he touches her hand, again.

"yeah," she chuckles, sadly, "right."

-c.h.

the parallels between loving someone and drug addiction
he remembered
the first time they kissed.
shaking hands.
her mouth.
sweet. new.
the brush of her tongue
against his lips.
experimentation.
he remembered
the first time he saw her naked.
sweaty skin.
her arching back.
beautiful. encompassing.
the taste of her
in his mouth for days.
addiction.
he remembered
the first time he told her he loved her.
tears on their cheeks.
her smile.
warm. pure.
the weight of her heart
in his hands.
dependency.
he remembered
the first time they fought.
trembling furniture.
her, crying.
horrible. sickening.
the pain of how she
didn't sleep next to him anymore.
withdrawal.
he remembered
the time she left.
opening drawers.
her suitcase, filled.

lifeless. cold.
the pit in his chest
where his heart used to be.
rehabilitation.
he remembered
the first time he was okay again.
sleeping.
not crying daily.
fine. okay.
hurting still but being
able to ignore it.
recovery.
he remembered
when they, were them.
damp sheets.
weak promises.
good. strengthening.
the absence of feeling
in his chest now.
recovered.

-c.h.

gravedigger

here lies all the sentences cut short by my indecisiveness
all the periods stapled on after words that weren't meant
to be the finish

i run my hands through frostbitten soil
and scrape my palms on headstones
where the bloodiest poems of mine are buried–
funny how each one is engraved with your name

and i will not apologize for writing about you
just like you will never apologize for making me
not because you aren't sorry
but because you don't realize that it's your fault

i didn't ask to be a poet
although it is my fault that i've let it ruin my life
i wish i could stifle the urge to bleed onto pages
i wish i didn't have to bury every sweet song
you had ever whispered in my ear

is this a love poem or an apology letter?
i can't tell the difference between them anymore–
mostly because i love you, but i'm sorry for it.

-c.h.

we are the new americana

we spend our days hiding liquor bottles under our car seats and cigarette packs in our nightstands and our grandparents scowl and tell us we are dooming the country but they always conveniently forget that their generation used dogs and firehoses to stop a protest that harmed nothing but their privilege and they shot a man on a hotel balcony just because he saw the unfairness in the web of society because it was always stickier where his people were stepping. we swallow pills to numb the pain more than we should and our parents scowl and tell us we are going to be destructive and selfish but they always seem to leave out the many times that their generation watched the gay boys get punched and knocked over in school and they never lifted a finger to help them because they thought that being heartlessly normal was better than helping someone who was different. we stay up until 3 am willingly and complain that we don't get enough sleep and we scowl at ourselves because we are going to be a horrible next generation but it's only because our ears take too many beatings from our hypocritical predecessors and our words are silenced by people who think that because they are grown they know exactly what is best for everyone even though history clearly shows they didn't. we may believe that we are going to be a horrible next generation but maybe that will be the reason we succeed, because even though we are destroying ourselves at least we aren't destroying other people.

-c.h.

stardust

i spend my nights tracing constellations on your skin, my finger finds the north star

but you *don't* say my name the same way anymore; the syllables seem to fumble around

on your tongue. i *know* people leave; that is what they are supposed to do after all,

and nobody knows the reason *why* we like to promise light years when we only plan to stay

seconds, you promised me a century, *i* made you my sun to try and convince you to give me

a little more time, but stars burn out and i *think* you don't kiss me the same anymore, your lips

feel all wrong, tight on my skin and cold. but maybe *i'm* wrong, maybe i overthink but my finger

finds the north star on your shoulder blade and i can't stop *losing* sleep over the thought that even the sun will die, i stare at constellations made of stars that are dead just like *you* and--

(i know why.)

(because i am.)

-c.h.

why i cried when you first told me you loved me

i am afraid. i am afraid of drowning in the depths of your blue irises but i am also afraid that if i do not take the plunge i will feel you slip away from me like sand between my fingers. i am afraid to let you light a fire in my heart but i am even more afraid that if you do not i will slowly melt from the inside out for it has been too long since someone with warm hands has touched me. i am afraid to love you but i am also afraid to lose you and to do one will prevent the other from happening at least for some time. i am afraid of being struck by the electricity in your fingertips i am afraid of being blown away by the power behind your words i am afraid of dying because of you. i am afraid of everything and nothing all at the same time because you make me quake with uncertainty and terror but you make my blood rush and my heart pound in the most delightful of ways because with you i think i am okay and i do not know if you feel the same. *i am afraid i am afraid i am afraid* because it is you who holds my heart in their palms and it is you who sometimes trips over their own feet and it is not me who decides when i am to be broken. i am afraid because you have the power to give me everything and take it all away at the same time.

-c.h.

to my love
you are unlike anything
i have ever known before
and as a poet
i am always looking
for new things
to write about

i can only hope
i will be writing about you
for a very long time

-c.h.

library of lovers
in my mind
sits a library.
the books in it
hold very special
tales; romances,
my romances.

sometimes i find
myself sitting in the library
when i'm tired or lonely,
brushing my fingers over
dusty books that have long
been closed.
sometimes, i even reach up
and pull one from the shelf,
open it and escape to what
once was.

there are small books that
take all of an hour to read;
they ended shortly, abruptly, even,
and they either left me wishing
it were longer,
or glad that it ended when it did.
there are large books,
the ones that take days or weeks
to get through.
these are the books i grew
attached to, and i was sad
when they came to an end.
at least, unlike the shorter ones,
they had time to develop,
and they didn't leave me
thirsty for more.
then there are the series,
the stories that were too long

and too intricate to be held within
one book.
these are the ones that i found myself
unable to put down, even when
they were finished.
the ones that i had been reading
for so long i didn't know what to do
once they were done.

there are many books
i have yet to read in this library.
there are some books i may
never open, depending on
where life takes me,
and some books
i never finished reading,
and put back on the shelf
before they ended.
 i have my favorites,
the ones i like to
skim through every
once in a while.

and then i have the
book i am reading now.

i have read many books
that have had sad endings,
or angry endings,
and ones that have hardly
had an ending at all.
i hope that for once,
this book ends happily,
and when it is finished,
i never have to read another
book again.

-c.h.

the healing process

the strangest thing about forgetting is what you still remember. little bits and pieces stay behind, while what you think would never leave you, disappear from your memory.

i can't remember your face. i can't hear your voice buzzing in my ear like it used to.

i can remember the color of your kitchen countertops; brown granite, like your eyes, but even then i can't recall the exact shade of your irises. i can remember how your house smelled on a Sunday, but i don't even remember the scent of your cologne.

there is a small clip of your laugh in the back of my mind. i'll reach in and press play sometimes, but each time it becomes more and more muffled, the audio skipping, skipping, skipping.

i remember every callous on your hand, every line, but i can't remember the way your lips curved up in a smile.

i can't remember your face, and every day, a little piece of you floats off and leaves me like you did.

i'll trace the outline of my collarbone like you did in hopes to see your ghost sometimes. but nothing comes.

i can't remember your face, because the mind blocks out traumatic events, traumatic people. my mind has blocked out your face, and maybe that's the most traumatic thing of all.

-c.h.

in the end i have to save myself
he says that he loves me
because he has to;
not because he wants to,
or needs to,
but because he has to.

as if i am a burden for him
that he can't leave out of fear
that i will not be able to carry myself--
as if i am dependent on him and
his half-hearted attempts to
make me feel happy.

he says;
but you need me, i cannot leave you.
i say;
i can learn not to need you,
for what is a bigger waste of time
than holding the hand of someone
who is a ghost of the love they used
to give you?

i tell him this;
for him to not love me and leave
would break my bones
and leave me breathless,
but for him to not love me and stay
would crumble me to dust
and render me unable to breathe
ever again.

                                        -c.h.

seeds

in 5th grade, my mother bought me my first bra. my chest was still plateaued, not yet molding into its womanly shape. i saw no point in it, as i thought i had no need to wear it yet, but my mother forced it on me and told me i was old enough that men would start staring. "it happened to me," she said.

in 6th grade, i held hands with a boy in the hallway and the teacher yelled at us until ears bled. i didn't understand what was so bad about enjoying how the blue-eyed boy's hand felt in mine. my teacher told me that it's best to avoid acting like that with boys until i was older, i could get mixed up with an older one who might have different ideas. "it happened to me," she said.

in 7th grade, i wore shorts to school one day that were a few inches above my knees. my science teacher took one look at me, shook his head, and sent me to the office to change. i didn't see what was so bad about my shorts; they were new and a pretty shade of red. the counselor who sat with my while i waited for my mother to bring a change of clothes told me that it was better not to wear clothes that give boys the wrong idea. "it happened to me," she said.

in 8th grade, i sat on my boyfriend's lap in class. he was in my chair and when he didn't move, i improvised. when my teacher walked in and saw. he screeched and told me to stay after class. i didn;t see what was wrong with joking around. he told me i should watch how i act with boys because they could view your actions as a silent yes. "it happened to me," he said.

in 9th grade, i let a boy get too close, too fast. his hands wandered my body like a map, a map he planned on throwing away. i didn't tell my mother. i didn't tell anybody. "it happened to them," i said, but my mouth stayed glued shut. i shouldn't have worn my push up. i shouldn't have kissed him so hard. i shouldn't have worn that tank top, those shorts. i shouldn't have laughed and weakly swatted at him when he pressed me against the well. i thought he was joking, i thought they were all joking. i kept my mouth shut, because it was my fault, wasn't it?

-c.h.

god, you did a fucking number on me

i keep calling you. can't stop calling. can't put the phone down. i get your voicemail every time and i cry because you don't sound angry at me on your voice mail. "hey, can't get to the phone right now, leave a message and i'll call you back." you sound good. happy. you sound like you're happy i'm calling and it doesn't make sense because everyone hears the same thing but to me it's like you're not sick of me. same voicemail after every call. it doesn't change. it doesn't transform into, "for fuck's sake can you stop calling me," or, "just leave me alone dammit," or, "i don't fucking love you anymore i told you," and i know it wouldn't do that but it's reassuring somehow that it doesn't anyway.

i ignore that my mother has threatened to take my phone if i don't stop. i ignore that my friends have stopped asking if i'm okay because what's the point if they know the answer won't ever fucking change. i don't listen to them because they don't know how it feels.

we aren't finished. i tell them that we aren't finished. you left with half the pages in the book still blank, so we must have another chance because why would you leave before the book was finished? they tell me that maybe i have to finish the book myself and i ignore them. i call you and listen to your voicemail some more.

i never leave messages. even when i'm drunk i don't leave messages. i just listen and hang up as soon as it beeps. i think this relieves my mother a little bit. last thing you want is a child that leaves their ex lover drunk messages.

 i know she's worried about me but i tell her i'm fine. this isn't her battle to fight and i don't want allies in this war. when i tell her not to worry she looks at me like a mother always looks at their child when they tell them they shouldn't worry. she tells me to stop calling you. i try to explain why i can't and she tries to explain the process of heartbreak and i'm angry because this isn't heartbreak. i'm not heartbroken, i'm just fucking broken. she doesn't get it. the older you get and the more secure you are in your marriage you forget what it felt like when the person you love more than anything leaves you and you have to teach yourself how to breathe and blink and eat again. i tell her this and she tries to take my phone. she tells me i have a problem and her nails scratch my skin. i am screaming and crying and clinging to my phone as if it were you and i am reminded of the night you left which only makes it worse. she gives up and tells me to leave. i run.

i go home and i call you twelve times. i don't expect an answer. i don't want one. but on the twelfth one, you pick up. you tell me to leave you alone. that you're going to change your number if i don't stop. that you don't love me anymore, and it's been six months so i should get the fuck over it and move on already. i act like it's your voicemail and don't say anything. i just listen. you hang up and i sit there and stare for an hour. i stare at the phone in my hands.

and i call again.

-c.h.

i've spent so long chasing after someone who doesn't care
my lungs crack like the ground in a drought
and i find it harder to
breathe
and breathe
and breathe

i have spent so long waiting for you
and i'm just now realizing that
you aren't coming back--
                    (why would you? i am so
                    small and unimportant)

in retrospect i may have been
a little too hopeful
considering you never gave a shit about me
                    (i just wanted you to so badly)

so i suck in mouthfuls of dust and swallow the sand
that's gathered under my tongue while i've stood here
not loving
not living
not breathing
for anyone else but you
                    (it's a wonder i didn't crumble to nothing)
                                        -c.h.

a series of short poems on the boys who love(d) me

1. you were my first everything
   and you ruined me you are
   why i have doubts about boys
   when they tell me they love me
   but we were young and stupid
   i've finally forgiven you
2. i kissed you to try and get
   over number one i stole your first kiss
   you said i was your first love too
   i didn't love you sometimes i think
   about your face when i told you the truth
   i have never stopped being sorry
1. when you came back i thought you'd
   changed you promised things were
   different i believed you because
   i had never stopped loving you and
   things were great until i realized you'd
   never stopped loving her either
3. you were sad and i thought i could
   save you but you can't just kiss
   depression away i will always regret
   giving up on you so soon but i am
   too selfish for someone as pure as you
   you deserve the best in the world and
   i thank you for finally forgiving me
4. i will always smile when i think of you
   there was nothing wrong with us you
   just can't fix something that was built
   already broken down i truly believe that
   you've never not belonged with her
   i was just a road stop on the way
5. i thought you were the end i meant
   every promise i ever made to you
   but instead of talking to me you were
   making out with girls you didn't care
   about and that's when you started to
   slowly break my heart
6. i wanted to show number five i could

kiss my friends for fun too i didn't mean
to fall in love with you i'm sorry i made you
want to kill yourself when i ended it but i
hope you've grown up because threatening
suicide won't make me love you again

5. i guess i didn't realize how much you loved
   me until you almost lost me to number six
   but we will never find someone who loves us
   as much as we love each other we are
   soulmates and you kissed another girl
   it doesn't matter you're my soulmate right

7. you were the kindest person i'd ever
   met you bought me gifts and told me
   i was pretty but you didn't like how
   i would shout my opinions and when i
   refused to change you left i learned that night
   that no boy is worth changing who you are

5. you had me wrapped around your finger
   and my heart locked in a cage you would stab
   it whenever i'd try to pull away so while
   you were kissing someone else i broke in
   and took it back after all those months
   i finally took it back

8. you've loved me for a long time and i'm
   sorry it took me so long to figure it out
   but i'm here now and i don't plan on leaving
   you are mine and i am yours forever and
   always i will love you for forever and always
   i promise i promise i promise

5. i finally get why you'd kiss other girls and
   not worry about losing me i now know what
   it's like to have someone love you so much
   you could do anything and they would stay
   the difference is that i wouldn't ever act on it
   i don't want to break him like you did me

5. i'm sorry i'm sorry i'm sorry i'm sorry i'm
   sorry i'm sorry i'm sorry i'm sorry i'm sorry
   i'm sorry i'm sorry i'm sorry i'm sorry i'm sorry
   i'm sorry i'm sorry i'm sorry i'm sorry i'm sorry

i'm sorry i'm sorry i'm sorry i'm sorry i'm sorry and i shouldn't be

5. do you realize now how much you meant to me how i had counted on us if you called for help i would still come to you if you needed a friend i would be there in a strange way you are still mine and i am still yours but we were never meant to be forever and always

-c.h.

ten things that told me you never loved me at all
1.four months in, i asked you, "do you know how i like my coffee?" and you frowned. "no," you said, "but i know when your birthday is. i remember the big things." but you forgot that i loved you, and that was the biggest thing of all.

2. after you first kissed me, you shrugged. i never understood the shrug until now. i was never more than a shrug to you, in the grand scheme of things, just a moment of 'i guess,' and to me, you were the epitome of 'absolutely.'

3. when i first said "i love you," you hesitated. you always hesitated with me. it was never the nervous kind, or the shocked kind. it was always the kind of hesitation when you don't mean what you're about to say. the kind of hesitation before you lie.

4. one time, i said, "baby, i'll always wait for you. if you ever have to leave, i'll wait for you to come back." you said, "okay."

5. when you left, you told me, "i never wanted it to be this deep. i never wanted you to fall in love with me. this wasn't supposed to be serious." i spent the next three months wondering if i was the problem; maybe i confused infatuation with love. but now i know that deep down, you were just angry at yourself. because you were telling the truth: you didn't want it to be this deep, but you let it happen. and knowing this doesn't make it any less painful.

6. you never once apologized for breaking my heart. not while you were leaving, when i was sobbing and telling you that breaking my heart was, in fact, exactly what you were doing. nor did you apologize in the months that followed. even now, i wait to hear from you. not because i still love you, but because i just want to know that you finally understand what you did. i don't think you ever will.

7. you never wanted to post pictures of me. or with me, frankly. you never brought me to any parties. when we hung out, it was always just us. maybe you were ashamed of yourself, but i always just thought i was an embarrassment. you never did anything to reassure me that i wasn't.

8. a month later, i texted you. "i just want to know if you're sorry. at all. even just the slightest bit. all i want is closure." you read it, and didn't reply, and that gave me my answer.

9. i saw you, once, at a party. alone. we spoke, briefly, and i said, "you let me waste half of a year on you. you could have stopped it before i was too far gone." you sighed, "i know i could've." i remember feeling so angry, so hateful. "then why didn't you?" and you looked at your feet, "i just kept hoping that i would feel something. anything. for your sake," and then you looked at me as if that equated to an apology. "you're full of shit," i spat, "you're not sorry. you loved the attention, and i bet you loved knowing that i was crying over you for months." you ran your hands through your hair, but you didn't say i was wrong.

10. four months in, i asked you, "do you know how i like my coffee?" and you frowned. "no," you said, "but i know when your birthday is." three weeks later, my birthday passed. and you forgot.

-c.h.

trans rights are human rights

society has taught us what we think is true;
girls like pink and boys like blue,
"there are no exceptions, no in-betweens,
there aren't any genders left unseen."

it's engraved into us since we've been born,
a patch in our mind that's not easily torn.
so when a boy likes dresses but a girl does not,
some can't understand; it's not what they were taught.

but not understanding is not an excuse
to be hateful or condescending; they're not just "confused."
they know who they are and they deserve respect,
they deserve happiness and acceptance, not anything less.

if "he" wants to be "she," you call them just that,
you don't fight or argue, you don't treat them like trash.
their pronouns are important and if you beg to differ;
sorry, you don't get to decide another one's gender.

who cares if it's "weird" or you don't know why,
it's not about what you think, it isn't your life.
you respect their decision because it doesn't harm you;
get over it: some boys like pink and some girls like blue.

-c.h.

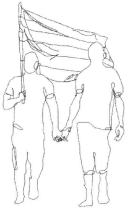

111

to those who claim they don't need feminism:
take a step back.
maybe a few steps back, for some of you.
take a step back out of your world and look at our world, the
world you're still a part of whether you'd like to be or not.
take a step back and listen to the bones crunching beneath your
feet.
the spines snapping under your toes.
the hair tangled in between your neatly trimmed fingernails.

look at our bodies.
our bodies, that we have bent and broken into a staircase for
you to walk up.
our bodies, that we have have torn and ripped to pieces so you
could use our limbs as a handrail.
our bodies, that have been branded with slurs and jeers that
you won't have to endure because of it.
this platform that you stand upon, this platform you think
makes you above the rest of us women who are still fighting,
who are still unsatisfied–
we built this for you.

you stand atop the skeletons of susan b. anthony, sojourner
truth, eleanor roosevelt, betty frieden, maya angelou, coretta
scott king.

tell me, would you tell these women that you don't need
them?
that you don't need their accomplishments? the rights they
fought their entire lives for? the rights they cried, yelled,
protested, and died for?
tell me, could you have done what they did?

without them, you would not be able to stand so tall.
without them, you would not be able to declare your strength
and independence.
without feminism, you wouldn't be able to say that you don't

need just that.

feminism.

we are not asking for you to lay down with us,
to take the blows as we do.
keep your primped hair and your manicured nails, and keep
your distance. some people will never be cut out to fight.
and that's okay. we have enough fight for all of us.
we just ask that perhaps, instead of shunning us and ignoring
history, you open your eyes, and maybe offer a bit of thanks.

-c.h.

untitled love poem (because i'm not sure what we are)
i think you'll taste like
sprite,
because something about
you is crisper,
sharper,
than just taking a bite
out of a peach.
there is more to you
than sugar.

and i think you'll feel like
springtime,
even the thunderstorms,
but i like the rain,
almost as much as i like
new beginnings and flowers.

most of all, though,
i think i'm falling in love
with you,
all the sour bites
and lightning strikes included.
i can shift my fingers through
the soil of us and feel the seeds
sprouting.

i hope they dig their roots
down deep.

-c.h.

twenty one days: a love story

day one: it's hot outside, simply sweltering, and there is sweat soaking through your shirt, but he has a friendly smile and warm eyes. "honestly, i'm sort of a bitch," you tell him. he nods, looks you over. "yeah, you look like one," he says, "but i don't mind."

day two: at lunch, you tell him you are in love with somebody. "i don't think he's real," he laughs, and when you ask why, he just shrugs. "i just don't think he is." you think you see sadness in his eyes.

day three: you watch how he moves, how his eyes crinkle as he smiles, how he frowns when his hair falls in his face. you remind yourself that you are in love with somebody. there is a jolt of pain in your heart.

day four: there are moments when the light catches his eyes and you feel your heart shake in its cage. "no," you tell yourself that night, "absolutely not."

day five: the stars look pretty tonight, but they are not the only beautiful thing you see. he tells you about a girl that broke him two years ago and you tell him about the boy that has yet to give back all the pieces. "can i say something?" he asks. "of course," you respond. he says, "i'm just really glad i met you." you go to bed smiling, and you hate yourself.

day six: your friend asks you if he loves you and you don't know what to say. "i'm in love with somebody else," you stammer, and they raise their eyebrows. "does he know that?" there is a pause before you respond, "yes, of course he does."

day seven: you are supposed to be in love with somebody, you tell yourself in the shower. there is a ring on your finger that serves as a reminder. in the shower, you cry. nobody can hear you above the sound of the water.

day eight: he reaches over and grabs your hand in the movie theatre. "no," you want to say, but you don't. you don't pull away, and you grip his hand even tighter. "i love him," you say later that night. "i know you do," he whispers, "but maybe you could love me too."

day nine: he wraps his arm around your waist. "you look beautiful," he murmurs to you and you hate yourself, you hate yourself for letting him say it and you hate yourself for loving the sound of his voice in your ear. "i can't do this," you start to cry, but he kisses your forehead. "yes you can," he argues, "you just shouldn't."

day ten: he asks you what you want to do. you look at his eyes, feel his hand burning into yours. "i'll be yours," you say, "but only for a little bit." he smiles, but it was never the answer he'd hoped for.

day eleven: you tell yourself that you don't love him, simply because you can't. at night, he tries to kiss you. you move so that he only kisses your cheek. "i can't," you say as you pull away. "and it's not just because i shouldn't. it's because i love him. i love him." you repeat it as you go to sleep, hoping you'd wake up and it'd be true again.

day twelve: you let him hold your hand and you try to numb yourself to the electricity shooting through your fingers. when he asks if you're okay, you smile and tell him, "of course." he squeezes your hand tighter, and you feel your throat close. when you run to the bathroom, his friend tells him that he's hurting you. he says, "i know. i know."

day thirteen: today you go out together. he asks you questions and you answer truthfully. he asks, "do you still love him?" you say, "i don't know anymore." then you grab his hand, and he smiles. at dinner he tells you he loves you, and you shake your head. "i know what you're thinking, but it's true." you rest your head on his shoulder and sigh. "i think, i think i love

116

you too."he kisses your fingers, "will you ever know for sure?" you stare at the table, "i don't know, maybe."

day fourteen: he cries today, and you feel panic spreading through you because you know it's your fault. "i'm tired of all the missed opportunities," he whispers, "you're going to forget about me." you grip his hand so tightly you know it hurts him. "i won't forget, even if it doesn't work out," you promise. "but that's the thing," he whimpers, "i don't want this to not work out." you almost kiss him, but you are supposed to be in love somebody else, and they are still lurking, in the back of your mind.

day fifteen: the bathroom tiles are swirling just like the toilet as you flush it again and again. you spend the day at the doctor and when you finally see him that night, he holds you even when you warn him that you're sick. "i was in a bad mood all day," he tells you, "and now i'm not. how strange is that?" you laugh and he tells you he loves you again. "i love you too," you reply, and for a few minutes, you forget.

day sixteen: "why won't you just kiss me?" he grabs your hands and pulls you close to him. "because," you say simply, "i should be in love with him." he runs his fingers through his hair, "but you're not anymore." you shake your head, "it's never that easy."

day seventeen: "i've never met someone like you before," he confesses. he runs his hand up and down your spine and you whisper sweet nothings in his ear. part of you wishes you don't mean it when you tell him you never want to leave, but all of you knows you do.

day eighteen: he is growing more and more upset as you get closer and closer to leaving. you write a poem about him in your journal, and he wants to see it but you tell him he'll see it later. "maybe i'll mail it to you," you joke, but he only looks sadder.

day nineteen: he asks, "we're going to be okay, yeah?" and you kiss his hand. "of course, angel," you say, "we'll be great, even." you say that you love him and he glows.

day twenty: when you kiss him, he freezes. he didn't see it coming. his hands rest delicately on your waist and for a few seconds there is nothing but him. he holds you afterwards and you can feel his smile against your neck. that night, he tells you how much he loves you a thousand times over. your heart cracks, not because you shouldn't love him, but because you do and time is up.

day twenty-one: you kiss him, hard, and cry into his shirt. you try to memorize the way his hands feel in yours, the way his lips feel against your skin. "we'll be okay," he mumbles into your hair, but his voice shakes and he is unsure. you are too. when you drive away, he watches and you start to cry again. "i love him," you sob, "i love him." you repeat it to yourself on the way home. but this time, you are talking about a different person.

-c.h.

conclusive
you ask
is the reason
you're so sad nowadays
because of me

i say
of course not

but i can feel the lie
licking at the back of my teeth

you ask
then why do you look
like you're about to cry
whenever you glance my way

i say
i don't know what
you're talking about

and i try to hide
that the tears are there
even now

you say
i may be pathetic
but i've never been blind

i look away and i confess
i don't think
we were ever meant
to fall in love

you stop speaking
and for a few minutes
we just sit

you smoke a cigarette
and i bite my nails

then you say
if we were never
meant to fall in love
then why did we

i don't have
an answer for this
but you take my silence
as one and let the smoke
float around us before you
speak again

i think we were meant
to fall in love but maybe
we weren't meant to fall
in love for forever

i say
this is heartbreaking

you say
well at least now
we know why it is

                              -c.h.

120

this is rape culture

she is 4. her cousin molests her and she is too young to do anything. she doesn't even know what's happening. when she tells people, later, they don't believe her.

they say, "why didn't you speak out about it sooner?"
fight back vomit. scream. she was a child.

she is 5. her step sister gropes her, uses her as a play thing. she doesn't process what happened until years later. she tells her dad. he says he doesn't believe her. says it isn't possible.
swallow. ignore the rising bile. she shouldn't have waited this long.

she is 6. her babysitter tells her they're going to play a game. slides her hand over her crotch. "i don't want to play," she says. "then you'll get in trouble," the babysitter replies, moves her hand closer. her parents ask her why she would want to ruin somebody's life. she wants to ask why they would let somebody ruin hers.
breathe. force down the words. she must have misunderstood.

he is 7. his uncle tells him to watch as he touches himself, tells him to touch himself too. when he finally figures out what happened, years later, his uncle is gone.
so he swallows it down. it doesn't matter now.

she is 9. her cousin pulls his pants down and begs her to touch him. rubs his hand on her through her underwear. his parents walk in on it.
they say, "boys will be boys. it's just what they do at this age."
choke it back. accept it. this is natural.

she is 10. her stepdad takes advantage of her. she is so scared to say anything that she doesn't. she finally works up the courage to speak. points at the places on the doll. the cops don't press charges.
they say, "it's a 'he said, she said' thing. sorry."
swallow. tremble. but why should they believe a child.

she is 12. she keeps telling herself it isn't happening. but it is, and he keeps doing it. she thinks she can trust him to not do it again. she's wrong. so she tells her mom.
she says, "you should've done something. you shouldn't have just frozen in place."
sob. pound the wall. she was too scared to do anything else.

she is 12. he takes her innocence, all of it. again and again. she sits, wide-eyed with trauma. she needs somebody to be there for her. it doesn't stop for three years.

121

they say, "you should've enjoyed the action."

they say, "you should learn from it."

swallow. see red. she was asking for too much.

she is 12. her best friend gropes her and doesn't stop. he won't listen. she tells her friends, hopes that they will understand. but they don't.

they say, "at least this means you're pretty."

they say, "this is just how boys are."

scream. swallow. at least she's desirable.

he is 14. he is gagged. his family member touches him and he can't scream. pushes his way inside. he can't scream for help. when he asks for it later, they don't understand.

they say, "it can't hurt that badly."

bite back the screams. sob. they won't get it, so they don't care.

she is 15. her boyfriend slips his fingers into her body. she tells him it hurts and he laughs. he keeps going. she stays with him because she doesn't know what else to do.

they say, "well why didn't you just leave him?"

swallow. choke. she should've just ran.

she is 15. her stepbrother rapes her, takes her for himself. when she tells the school, he is kicked off the football team for a week. he still walks free and she is permanently chained to a memory she never asked for.

swallow. swallow. she doesn't matter.

she is 15. a football player offers to walk her to class. he pulls her around the corner and gropes her, pins her against the wall so she can't move. she goes to administration and they try to give her a detention because she went with him. he didn't get anything.

swallow. sob. she's the problem.

she is 16. he is 23. he gets her drunk and traps her against the wall, blocks out her protests with his mouth on hers and a hand up her dress. he takes what he wants.

they say, "that's why you don't drink."

they say, "if it really happened, she wouldn't tell anybody. it's too embarrassing."

swallow. chew on words. she's at fault for this.

he is 16. his boyfriend holds him down and masturbates on to him. "i know you want it," he growls. says he has to win him back, tears away his clothes. he threatens to scream, and the boyfriend tells him he never wanted him back, just wanted to see how far he could get him to go.

they say, "you were being a bad boyfriend."

they say, "we don't believe you," and they leave.

dry heave. hit the wall. why is he surprised.

she is 17. she is drunk. she tells him she wants to go to bed. "okay, then go to bed," he says, and slides his fingers into her anyway.

they say, "he's such a cool guy, though. you probably did something that made him think it was okay."

choke on the air. swallow. she should've just kept her mouth shut.

i am 18. i can still feel his hands on my chest. his prints are branded into my skin. i don't like to look in the mirror anymore. i want to scream.

but i know what they say.

swallow. swallow. choke.

i know what they say.

so i don't say anything at all.

-c.h.

the boys i've loved and the end of the world #4
"it's going to consume the earth. a giant light ball, and it's
going to swallow the earth whole."

we are walking, in his town, a town i've never been to until
now. our arms swing side by side, sometimes brushing, and the
sun is beaming calmly down on us. "i still find it hard to
believe that the sun shining on us now, is the same sun that will
kill everyone and obliterate the planet in three days," i say with
a slight laugh.

"i still find it hard to believe that i'll never get a chance to
marry you," he responds, and i hit his arm, but i am laughing
and so is he.

"maybe in heaven, you will," i giggle, and he rolls his eyes.

"please, we both know it's not real," he scoffs, but he looks at
me and his eyes are scared. i know, that if i could see mine in a
mirror, they would be, too. he grabs my arm, stopping us. "tell
me, was it always the distance that pushed you away?"

i nod, and my chest feels heavy. "of course it was. it's always
distance, isn't it?" i sigh, knowing that every promise i made to
him, won't matter in three days' time. "i wish it hadn't been
there."

he draws me closer, wraps his arms around me, and i let him. i
will never feel them again after today. "i wanted to give you
the world," he whispers, "ever since i first saw you, i wanted to
give you everything i had. you were it for me."

i bury my face into his chest and say nothing. but he knows i
feel the same. he's always known, and he'll go to his death
knowing it, crumbled to ash by the broken sun.

"i hope he knows how lucky he is to be loved by you," he

murmurs into my hair, "i hope he knows that he's holding a star brighter than the sun in his arms."

i am crying now, and i clutch his jacket tight. "i have never been more sorry about anything," i confess, "there is nothing that hurts more than knowing we will never get a chance."

"if heaven is real, please promise you will find me there." he cups my face in his hands, forcing me to look up at him.

"i promise. i promise, i promise, i promise."

with a sigh, he presses his lips to my forehead. "good. i cannot bear the distance any longer."

-c.h

the aftermath
people say it's possible
to die from a broken heart.
before you,
i didn't believe it.

but then you left.

and suddenly,
i couldn't breathe.
i found myself
sitting in the shower,
choking on boiling water
and watching my skin
blister red.

suddenly,
there was a gaping
hole in my chest.
i would find myself
hunched over the toilet
and heaving up what
little food i could manage
to eat.

there were days
where i could hardly
manage to get out of bed.
when my limbs would shake
and i would have to think
about each step before
i took it.

i still don't believe
that it's possible to die
from a broken heart.

but i know now
that it's possible to feel
like you are.

-c.h.

this is why you hold on
she's dug her grave, she's written her will,
her eyes are closed, she's swallowed the pills.
she's scribbled her note, she's said goodbye,
she's very certain, she wants to die.

she's in the hospital, her stomach is pumped,
she's laying in the bed, a sad sick lump.
her hair is knotted, her words are few,
her parents are crying, nobody knew.

she's grown up now, her wounds are healed,
her eyes are bright, her smile is real.
she lights up with laughter, she's glad she stayed,
she's ever so grateful, she lived another day.

-c.h.

resolve
i will never understand
why everything could never
be enough for you.

i tried to give
you all i had.
i thought i did.

now that it's over
and it no longer
hurts, all i am
able to say is
that i want you
to be happy, though
i know you won't.

you will always be
searching for something more.
perhaps at some point,
you will realize that
with me, you had
it all. all that
you had ever wanted.

i doubt it will
come to that, and
i know all you
wanted was true love.
i'm sorry you didn't
think i could give
you that. i promise
that i tried to.

this is my goodbye.
you will always be
in my heart, darling.

one day, we may
meet, and try again.
one day, you may
realize that you still
miss me, and you
will finally know why.
i want all this.

but most of all,
one day, i hope
that you will have
found what it is
that you're looking for.

-c.h.

thought process
i think
that maybe
i was in love
with you
but i didn't
want to be

i think
that maybe
you deserved
someone who
didn't always look
away when you smiled
in their direction

i think
that maybe
i drove you
away from me
not because
i was too much
but because
i was too little

i think
i fucking
ruined us

i think
i am a
disaster

i think
i am hard
to love

i think
i know
why we fell
apart and
i think
i know
that it was me

i think
i'm not making
excuses for why
you left
because i want
to think you loved
me but
deep down
i know i am

                              -c.h.

it was there the second i stepped into the room. the tension. it soaked the air, so thick i could have sworn i would have been able to press my fingers into it had i tried. it didn't take long for me to figure out why-- although i did see it coming.

i knew he would be here.

i found it cruel, cruel of whoever, or whatever, was in charge of fate, to bring us together again. not here. this, of all places, was the most haunted. when our eyes met, i knew he was thinking the same thing.

it took all i had to walk towards him, and it felt like i was stepping on glass shards the entire time. with every inch, another memory blasted itself into my mind. i could see the ghosts of us, i could feel his touches, and even now, they made my heart stop. which, more than anything, was what made it so terrifying.

and then, i was standing in front of him. he looked the same; a little sadder, maybe, but i suppose i was wearing the same broken expression.

he spoke first, just like he always did. "hi."

the single syllable jarred me. i let his voice wash over me like melted gold-- it was always one of my favorite things about him. after a few seconds, i managed to reply. "hi. i didn't expect to see you here." a lie, of course, and he knew it.

but he chose to ignore it. "how have you been?"

"good," i told him, and it was the truth: i had been good, great, even, but being here, with him, was starting to pick away at my progress. i could feel it decaying, and it had only been a few minutes. "what about you?"

133

"better, i've been better," he answered, and then he gestured to the seat next to him. "would you like to sit?"

no. but i did, and the fight within me died quickly as i registered just how close we were. closer than we had been in months. almost as close as we had been before. my heart pounded.

he could tell i was a disaster; i had always been bad at hiding my emotions. but i knew him, almost better than i knew myself, and i could see him cracking. every glance i cast towards him sent another fragment falling to the ground. he was already in pieces-- my handiwork, of course.

finally, he cut through the fragile silence. "i just, um... i guess i wasn't as prepared for, for... this," he said, slowly, as if he were handpicking every individual letter.

"yeah," i agreed, as carefully as him, "it's... it's a lot harder, than i, i thought it would be."

"does that mean that--" he stopped himself. i wanted to press him, tell him to finish it, but when i looked at him, his eyes finished it for me.

the hope.

does that mean that you still love me? he was asking. *does that mean we still have a chance?*

"no." the word tasted like acid on my tongue, and i almost choked it out, "it just means it still hurts."

"i'm sorry," he whispered, and i hated it. hated to see him like this, so quiet and cracked. hated to see us like this, the exact opposite of what we were. we became what we promised we never would: strangers.

"i know you are. and i-- i'm trying to forgive you, i am. but it's hard. and this, this is hard." the truth. it always seemed to come out so easily around him. i never understood it. "i want us to be able to be friends," i confessed, "like we were before. because i was your friend first. and i loved that." *almost as much as i loved you,* i finished in my head.

he ran a hand through his hair. "i don't-- i don't know. i don't think i'm okay yet. everything hurts still, you know? and there are days where i'm fine but then something reminds me of you or you show up in a dream and everything just hits me like a brick, that i had you, and now i don't, and i caused it--" he was rambling, and he knew it, but it didn't stop him, "i mean, even this, this is killing me right now," his voice shook, "and i don't know when i'm going to be able to look at you and--and not love you."

i said nothing, because there was nothing to be said. i knew all of this. he'd told me a thousand times; begged for me to come back, and each time, i said no. i had to. for myself, and for him. we were breaking each other.

"i just wish... i just wish i could do it all over again." his hand grazed mine, and i flinched. across the room, the ghosts of us sat together, fingers intertwined, heads huddled close together in a tender conversation. they had no idea of what was to come. i remembered how sweet it all was, and the taste seemed to wash over my mouth like syrup.

he touched my hand again, and i jolted away from the past. it was over, and i couldn't do anything to change it.

but i could do something now.

his fingers brushed against mine, and i faced a dilemma.

i could push him off, and walk away. close this door for good. i couldn't let it stay as it was; left slightly ajar, inviting him inside, but never completely. he always had to push a little. but i could also take the jump. i could reach out and take his hand, and we could try again. i could see it in front of me. i knew we loved each other. and sitting in the place where it all began, remembering how gentle and soft it had been, i wanted to believe that we could resurrect it. that we could learn from our mistakes, and we could make it.

but i also remembered what tore us apart. his arrogance, and my paranoia. his selfishness, and my tendency to go the self-preservation route. his secrets, and my hypocrisy. the lack of communication, and the distance. of course, always the distance.

i looked down at his hand, and up into his eyes.

"take it," he pleaded, his blue eyes glistening, "please. we can do it."

and i did. i let my fingers intertwine with his and for a second a warmth washed over me. i looked around, and i saw the ghosts around us. us, kissing in the corner. us, cuddled on a bench. us, happy, unbroken. and for a moment, i couldn't differentiate between my memories and the present.

which was the problem.

i pulled my hand back, ignoring the cold, sick feeling puddling in my chest. he looked shattered. "why?"

"because," i said, "because when we're here, we're haunted by what we were. all we see in this place is the beginning of us, the part of us that wasn't torn or broken or poisoned. and we can't go back to that. we just-- can't. you've hurt me too many times. lied to me, made me cry. and i've hurt you, made empty promises and then walked them back, left you behind while i moved on. we can't get this," and i gestured to our past, "back. it's impossible. we're broken. and we need to, we need to be with people who can fix us. and that isn't what we are for each other. that's just... that's just the way it is." i stood. "i'm sorry, i am. but we can't keep falling into this trap. you're not moving on because you keep thinking there's a chance for us. but there isn't. and i hope that, that hearing it from me, helps you break away from this, whatever it is."

"but, i love you," he murmured, looking down at his hands. they were speckled with tears. "isn't that enough?"

"no. not anymore." i felt tears gathering in my eyes. it hurt to say it. it hurt so, so much. but i had to. "i'm so sorry. but you'll be okay. i know you'll be okay. i have to do this. it's the only way."

"only way for you," he snapped, and although it was soft, it was laced with anger.

"no. it's the only way for you." i turned. "you may not see it right now, but one day, you'll thank me for this. i couldn't let myself keep breaking you." and then i was gone, walking swiftly out the door.

as i left, the ghosts of us swirled around me, and i took one last look over my shoulder. he had left. in his place, was the apparitions of two broken lovers; he reaches for her hand, and she walks away with the shattered determination of someone who was fighting not to turn around.

"thank you," i breathed, to nobody but the air.
"thank you for showing me how to save myself."

-c.h.

137

autopsy

sometimes, i get into ruts where i relive
all of my relationships
and i dissect them
as though they were frogs
in anatomy class.

i peel back the surface
as though it were a layer of skin
and then i pick my way
through the insides of each one
and i try to make myself
understand again where it went wrong.
what it was that made the heart stop beating.
as if understanding why it died
would resurrect it
so i could maybe give
a couple another chance.

i especially spend a lot
of time digging through
the corpse of us.
each time, it is
more rotted than the last.

and as the organs shrivel
and the bones begin to crumble
i find out more about us.
i pull out lies from between the ribs
and the things we left unsaid from its stomach.
in its heart, i discover that it was
broken long before it stopped beating.

at some point,
i will have torn our remains
apart.

much like we did
to each other.

-c.h.

soulmates

my first soulmate was for the young me, the innocent me, the i need somebody to call me beautiful or else i won't believe it me, the i'm too young to understand the complexities of relationships me, the please just kiss me and call me pretty me. he was for the me that thought i was broken because a boy didn't have a crush on me back, the me that didn't know what being broken felt like, the me that didn't know what being broken even meant. he was the soulmate for the me that had never been kissed, never been in love, never been whispered pretty promises to, never been lied to, never been cheated on, never been heartbroken. and when i had experienced these things, he was no longer my soulmate. he was first love.

my second soulmate was for the transforming me, the temporary me, the i'm working on getting over the first soulmate me, the i'm still not over it me, the i still don't understand how relationships work but i'm getting there me. he was for the me that needed a friend, the me that let myself fall in love with anybody who wanted me to, the me that didn't get the work it took to make things, well, work. he was the soulmate for the me that had too high of expectations, too little dedication, too many cracks that i put in myself. and when i had learned what i need to learn, he was no longer my soulmate. he was fragile love.

my third soulmate was for the strong me, the i love myself me, the i am finally good to myself me, the i don't really care if you want me at all because i'm fine without you me, the but it would be nice if you did want me back me. he was for the me that wasn't sure where to go but just knew not to go backwards, the me that had figured out that boys aren't worth hurting yourself over, the me that knew that and still hurt herself over boys. he was the soulmate for the me that still searched for somebody else, the me that was never quite satisfied with what i had, the me that should have been satisfied, the me that should have stopped looking. and when i didn't stop looking, he was no longer my soulmate. he was selfish love.

my fourth soulmate was for the broken me, the careless me, the
i really think you're my soulmate me, the i know you're
hurting me but i don't care me, the he has to be the one me. he
was for the me that gave up everything for one little taste, the
me that allowed toxicity due to circumstance, the me that believed
the promises made and the words said, the me that stayed up waiting
for you to come back long after i knew you wouldn't. he was the
soulmate for the me that needed to go back to being strong, the me
that needed to open her eyes, the me that needed to realize when
something had ended. and when i realized it, he was no longer my
soulmate. he was toxic love.

my fifth soulmate is for the new me, the brave me, the i'm
going to kiss you when you least expect it me, the i'll text you
ten times in a row and not give a shit me. he is for the me that
is now, the me that lives and breathes light, the me that is no
longer bound by chains. he is the soulmate for the me that i
love, the me that i am, the me that i have always been. and now
that the young, the transforming, the strong, the broken, and
new parts of me know this, we can settle. we can breathe. and
we can stop looking. for we have found it. he is unconditional
love.

-c.h.

out of habit
i tore stars from my veins for you
spit up my dreams into your outstretched hand
wiped the corner of my mouth and smiled through the burning in
my throat.
you tapped the lock on my chest
and i should have known then that nothing would ever be enough
for you.
but i handed you the key because for once i was determined
to not let the voices in my head get the better of me.

i told myself that i had to stop ripping my relationships apart at the
seams
so i let you rip me apart instead.
in the end i don't think my love was unrequited
but i do think it was unappreciated.
i want to think that you had no idea what you were doing
but i know you saw me the day after
and i also know that you never apologized.

love is cynical and honest
i tell myself that it only wants what's best for me
yet i keep finding myself bearing my back
handing them the knife
closing my eyes
looking the other way.
trying to convince myself that the gashes on my skin came from a
stranger
and not the person i slept next to.

i'm starting to wonder if maybe love is trying to teach me a lesson
and i have just refused to learn it.

-c.h.

the boys i've loved and the end of the world #5

"i can't believe i'm going to die young," he says, his arms folded around me, "i thought i was going to grow old and have kids and pay taxes."

"nothing ever turns out as planned, does it?" i say, tired. we are waiting, tangled up in sheets and blankets and our own bodies.

"i guess, spending the end of the world with you isn't so bad," he jokes, and i kiss him. he is warm and tastes like sunlight, if it had a flavor, the kind that didn't destroy planets and burn everything to nothing.

"what if we're already dead, and we don't know it. it happened so fast that we didn't even feel anything, so this is heaven."

"what if, you're just crazy." i raise my hand to hit him, but he catches it and holds it in his own as he kisses me again. "i thought we'd have more time," he says sadly.

outside, the sky is glowing. i look at the clock and it's eleven at night. the end is coming.

"i thought we would, too." he holds me tighter and we watch the sky. it's beautiful, and i smile.

the wind starts to beat against the walls, and i can feel it getting closer, ripping up the ground.

"i always hoped we would last," he yells over it all, and he is crying, and so am i, but even now he is beautiful, and i want to kiss him.

"we lasted until the end of the world, didn't we?" i shout, and he laughs, a carefree, happy sound, and i cherish it, knowing i may never hear it again.

the wind grows louder and the glass in the windows start to crack. i kiss him, hard, and he pulls the blanket over us.

for a moment, there is nothing but the two of us and the sound of our heartbeats.

then, there is nothing but light.

-c.h.

excerpt from the story of us

"i'm giving up on you," she declared, ignoring the way her voice shook and her stomach plummeted as she said it. "i'm giving up on you, not because i want to, but because i have to. for both of us. you don't love me anymore, and i know this now. i've been holding out hope that maybe there was something there, something lingering, but i've figured it all out."

she held his gaze as best she could, looking past the pain in his eyes, the protest blooming on his lips. "when we met, we didn't know what would happen," she continued, "we didn't know the people we'd meet or the things that would happen. we had no clue. we tried to predict it by betting on our futures being each other, but you can't gamble with fate. fate will always win. i put, i put my whole heart into you–us, and look how that turned out," with that, she laughed, all dry and broken. "but none of that matters now. you chose otherwise. and i did, too. i'm not free of blame, here."

he tried to speak, reach out to her, but she pushed his hand away, quieting him. "i fell in love with him because i thought… i thought we weren't an option anymore. because you were always gone, gone when i wanted you and gone when i needed you. i tried so hard to keep us alive. i ignored the fact that the writing on the wall was no longer just writing; it was carved into the plaster. i blocked out what my friends said, because they didn't know us, they didn't know you. but what they did know was that with every day that passed, i cracked more and more. they could see it on my face, in my actions, in the way i talked about you. fuck, they realized you were breaking me long before i did."

"i'm sorry," he whimpered, "i'm so sorry, just please–"

"no," she whispered, and her eyes clouded with tears, "don't you see? i can't. you can't take back what you did to me. i needed you, you fuck. more than anybody else, i needed you. and you weren't there. she wasn't just a friend, and it wasn't just a kiss, and you knew it too. but you lied, and dragged me along because you knew i was so hurt i wouldn't have the strength to leave."

she smiled, suddenly, "but he had the strength. and he saved me, and he opened my eyes. to the reality of what we were. he gave me everything i ever wanted from you– and i never asked for much. and more. he gave me so much more, things i never dreamed of with you. so you can't blame me for falling in love with him. you can't blame me for getting tired."

"but you promised–"

"i know what i promised, and i tried to keep it. i really, really did. you were the one that fell through. you were the one that stopped replying. you were the one that left my messages ignored. you were the one that wasn't there to congratulate me on my accomplishments, or comfort me on my failures." she paused, and although her voice trembled, she felt stronger now before him than she ever had before. "but me? i kept the conversations going. i asked you how your day was. i was your biggest fan and the best friend you could have ever fucking had, even after all the shit you threw at me. but none of that seemed to matter to you, so i finally got it. i finally understood what the lack of replies meant."

"and what," he murmured, "did it mean?"

"it meant," she said simply, "that it's time to give up on you. i don't think you really want me around anymore, now that i'm not in love with you. i'm not a pretty girl you can show off to boost your ego. i never was. i was more than that, or at least i was supposed to be. i deserved more. and i got it. after all this time, i got it. and just because that hurts your fucking feelings," she pointed her finger at his face, her eyes sparked with anger, "doesn't meant i'm going to throw it all away. so i'm giving up on you, finally. i'm sorry that i wasn't worth your time until i didn't want it anymore."

-c.h.

reincarnate

i think in our previous lives, we've always been in love with
each other, estranged and held apart by a thin thread.

you were the king's son and i was a peasant girl.
i was an aristocrat and you worked in the stables.
i was in love with somebody else.
you were in love with somebody else.

the first time we met, the world must have stopped in its tracks.
because when i first saw you in this lifetime, i felt everything
freeze.

we have always loved each other from afar, each lifetime
drawing us closer and closer.

the first time, you accepted a flower from me when you were
riding through my village. you rode through it often, and one
time you stopped, got down from your carriage, and spoke to
me. but you were soon married to a princess, just like all
princes were.
the second time, you helped me learn how to ride and take care
of my horse. sometimes our hands would brush when we
groomed him together. you were my confidant. my friend. we
never once told each other what we really felt.
the third time, you were my neighbor, my best friend, and one
night you kissed me during a game of hide and seek. "i love
you," you'd said to me, and for a second i loved you too. but a
few weeks later i started dating somebody else. that summer,
you moved away. in that lifetime, i broke your heart.
the fourth time, we had each other, for a while. our families
vacationed by the same lake. you didn't tell me you had a
girlfriend until you had seen everything i had to offer you. you
watched me cry in front of you. your family left the next day. in
that lifetime, you broke mine.

our souls knew each other before we did. they found each other from across the room and pulled us together. "it's you," they said to one another, "i'm so glad it's you. maybe we can get it right this time." and then it began, again.

this time, we could have made it if we had had the strength. the courage. but i was afraid and your heart wasn't there. eventually, mine wandered too. we drifted, our souls still reaching out for each other even though our hands no longer were.

but this time, we knew.
this time, we told each other.
this time, we fought.

in this lifetime, there wasn't an issue of who broke who.
in this lifetime, we merely broke each other.

i know it's heartbreaking to think we never got a real chance. your sobs ring as loud in my ears now as they did the day we shattered, and they haunt me.

our time in this life together is over. we lost this round.
but each lifetime, we inch closer and closer.

and in my heart, i hope.
my soul, it longs for you still.

it has picked itself out of the rubble of yet another failure and pieced itself back together.

my soul, it knows.

"i will find you again," it whispers into the cosmos, "there are many lifetimes to come."

from across the world, your soul returns,
"we will get our chance yet."

-c.h.

among the gray
i watch our story on rewind
in black and white.

sometimes i wish i could
see the blue of your irises
but i don't think i'll ever be able
to picture us in color again.

i don't love you anymore,
i know better than that now,

but i still find myself writing about you
late at night when i forget how to breathe
and it's like,

how do i learn to breathe again
without it being because of you?

i traded a kind love for a powerful love,
and you gave me it--

i still find traces of you in every damn thing,
the backseat of a car and the booth of a restaurant,
i guess in a way we're lasting like we said we would,
and you know,

i think about you on friday nights
when my friends are out drinking and i'm sitting at home
writing this stupid fucking book about you
because for some reason i can still trace the shape of your mouth
with my finger in the mirror, even now,

and i don't think i love you anymore
because it's not that i miss you, it's not that i want you back,
it's just that i still have to justify why i'm always looking for
skeletons in their closet, i still leave the door open because
i don't want to make their awaited exit any more painful,

and the thing is, the reason why i can't stop writing about you,
is that despite the cracks in my cheeks and the way my hands shake

when i touch his chest, how i can't seem to stop looking over my shoulder,

i still don't regret a single fucking thing.

-c.h.

a year in review

december 31st, 2015, 10:23 pm: i saw you for the first time. you were talking to a girl and i could tell that you were capturing her with every syllable that left your mouth. and i knew why: you were beautiful and bright, and i was drawn to you even then, like the planets are drawn to the sun.

december 31st, 2015, 11:58 pm: we met standing in line for the bathroom. you introduced yourself, and asked for my name, smiling when i gave it. "lovely," you murmured, and repeated it a few more times, rolling the letters around in your mouth like a new food.

january 1st, 2016, 12:05 am: i could still feel you on me, your lips, minutes, hours, months later. the clock had struck midnight and you just grabbed me, didn't ask if it was okay until it was over. you were laughing, brushing it off, all teeth and well-kissed lips, but i knew i saw you blushing.

january 21st, 2016, 1:12 pm: you got my number through the mutual friend that threw the party. i still don't know how you got my address. i didn't remember telling you. you couldn't tell me, either.

february 14th, 2016, 9:12 pm: you took me out to dinner and bought me chocolate and roses. it was all so cliché, and i loved every second of it. when you kissed me good night, i swore i could feel the rest of my life, pressed right up against my lips.

february 26th, 2016, 11:33 pm: we made it official. i remember how you asked me, how shy you got, like you didn't know what the answer would be.

march 17th, 2016, 5:43 pm: we spent the day at the saint patrick's day parade, and you filled yourself with beer and kissed me hard against the bar bathroom door. i drove you home and that was the first time you told me you loved me.

march 18th, 2016, 9:24 am: you called me and told me you loved me again. "i want to make sure that you know i still mean it when i'm sober," you said.

march 24th, 2016, 1:09 pm: i met your parents at easter brunch. you had demanded i come with you, and i was glad i did. your mother was kind and beautiful, and your father was warm and handsome, just like i knew they'd be. after we'd eaten, your mother got me alone. "he's never brought a girl home before," she told me, "normally he isn't very open about who he's dating. but you, you're different. don't read into this, but i think he may really think you're special."

april 12th, 2016, 8:31 pm: you saw me naked for the first time, and you kissed every inch of my skin. i'd never felt that much love from anybody before that night, and i haven't since. not even you could replicate those few hours.

may 5th, 2016, 4:57 pm: we fought for the first time. i ran into my ex at the grocery store and wanted to chat for a few minutes. you didn't. when we got in the car, you told me that if i was still in love with somebody else i could just leave, and i told you that you should trust me and not be so insecure about our relationship. we screamed the whole way home and you slammed the car door when i dropped you off. i almost crashed three times on the drive home.

may 6th, 2016, 8:03 am: you came by with flowers and breakfast. "i'm sorry," you told me, "you just mean so much to me, and the thought of you ever being anyone else's makes me sick." i smiled, "but you don't have to worry about that now. i'm yours."

june 16th, 2016, 10:51 pm: for my birthday, you took me out to dinner and gave me a beautiful necklace with a silver chain and pearl pendant. we drank expensive wine and stumbled back to my place and fucked. i had never been fucked before, not like this. i woke up the next morning with bite marks on my neck and hickeys all the way down my stomach, but you were gone. "had to run," you'd written on a post it note, "i love you."

june 18th, 2016, 2: 41 pm: i hadn't seen you since my birthday and you weren't picking up when i'd call.

june 19th, 2016, 3:13 am: "had to run," the post it note had said. maybe you were running from me. i couldn't tell if it was the 3 am darkness talking or the part of me that already knew.

july 1st, 2016, 4:01 am: i looked over at you, sleeping in the darkness beside me. when we were together, things felt perfectly normal. but now, i could feel the shifts. "are we falling apart?" i whispered to you, and although i hadn't expected an answer, the silence broke my heart all the same.

july 4th, 2016, 6:47 pm: we were at a barbecue and i saw you across the crowd, talking to a girl. i saw the way she was drinking up every word that escaped from between your lips, and that's when i knew. that's when i knew you weren't mine anymore.

july 21st, 2016, 7:08 pm: i brought it up to you. "i think we're starting to grow apart," i said, "there's a distance between us that wasn't here before." you reassured me that it was all in my head, but i didn't hear it in your voice. i didn't see it in your eyes. you knew it was there, too, but unlike me, you weren't trying to do anything to stop it.

august 10th, 2016, 11:37 pm: i lay awake and thought about what your mother said, all these months later. "don't read into this." but of course i did. i couldn't help myself. fuck, i loved you so much.

august 15th, 2016, 1:12 pm: you invited me over and i discovered that the key you'd given me no longer worked. "i had the locks changed," you said, "i'll get you a new one." it was a lie, and i knew it. you didn't get me a new key.

september 8th, 2016, 2:00 pm: i caught you cheating. in a desperate attempt to revive the romance we'd had at the beginning of our relationship, i bought dinner and brought it to your place. when you finally opened the door, i saw it written all over your face; the way your eyes widened, the way your jaw dropped, the way your cheeks drained of color. i heard it in the stammer of your voice, the sharp intake of your breath, the grinding of your teeth. when the girl walked up behind you, half naked, asking who it was at the door, i already knew. "how could you?" i whispered, and you just opened and closed your mouth. the girl pieced it together and started screaming. she hadn't known. i left the food at the doorstep.

september 10th, 2016, 1:49 am: you never called after that, never came by, never reached out, but it wasn't like we'd needed to confirm anything. i knew it was over, but it took every ounce of willpower i had not to go back to your place and find out why, why everything.

september 27th, 2016, 6:20 pm: i kept finding myself huddled in a ball; in my bedroom, in my kitchen, in my shower. not crying, or yelling. just huddled, clutching my body close to myself, staring. still not understanding.

october 31st 2016, 9:01 pm: i spent halloween haunted by the ghost of you. your face was around every corner. i could still feel your touch trickling down my spine. that night, i lost it. the anger surged through the sadness and bubbled to the surface. i screamed until my throat was raw, screamed at nothing, about nothing, for no reason other than i was too full.

november 10th, 2016, 2:17 am: you called me when you were drunk and i answered. i listened to you ramble, vomiting up apology after apology. near the end, you told me you loved me. "call me tomorrow when you're sober if you still love me," i said. you didn't.

november 25th, 2016, 7:15 pm: i went out on a date with somebody new. they didn't pull me in like you did, but for a few hours, i forgot about you and i felt okay. i drank myself to sleep that night so i wouldn't have to think about you. the next morning, the hangover hurt more than you did. it was a start.

december 24th, 2016, 8:12 pm: i was spending christmas with my family, and i was doing great until my aunt asked about you. i told her you cheated, but i was doing okay, and then i excused myself and threw up the appetizers into the toilet. i called you then, and when you picked up, i let out a sob. "you ruined me, you fuck," i croaked, "and you can't even apologize. not when you're sober, at least." there were a few seconds of silence, and then you hung up. i still hope that it ruined your christmas.

december 31st, 2016, 10:23 pm: i saw you for the first time in months across the crowd. it made me sick to know that even after all that had happened, you were still the most beautiful person in the room to me.

december 31st, 2016, 11:55 pm: you found me in the kitchen. "i wanted to tell you i'm sorry," you yelled over the music, "and i miss you." and in those final moments of the year, i thought about it. i thought about letting you back in. the countdown started, and you moved closer to me. and i.. i pushed you away. i turned away from you and said, "no. i can't." and i walked out of the room.

january 1st, 2017, 12:05 am: i have forgotten how you felt against me, your lips. and for the first time, i am finally okay with that.

-c.h.

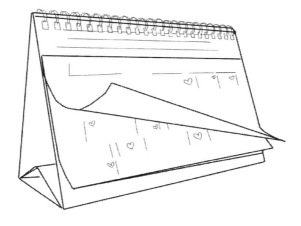

the train is coming
so i kiss you
goodbye at the
station

some things
are not meant to last

forever

i leave you
because i
have to

i leave you
like i was
always meant
to go.

                              -c.h.

now that we've reached the end
i hope you know that
you are the only one
i will never write
sad love poetry
about

because when we ended
my heart was more whole
than it had been
in the beginning

                    -c.h.

and until we meet again
i stand here at the precipice.
i do not want to be one who looks back at high school
as if they were the best times of my life.
the best, for me, has yet to come.
but the best times of my life so far have often happened within
the white-bricked walls of your classroom.

sicut erat--
since the beginning.
since the beginning of music there have been people like you,
people who love and cherish every note, every syllable.
i have always wanted to be one of the masters,
and these last four years i have been learning from the best.

i stand here at the precipice.
the world awaits me.
the music of my future is calling.
i look back upon the music of my past,
and you.

go, you say. *go and make the best*
of this messed up world.

thank you, i reply.
thank you for reminding me i have a voice
on the days where i could barely make a sound.

-c.h.

the boys i've loved and the end of the world, epilogue
i wonder if they will all be here, the boys i've loved, wherever we are now.

i wonder if i will see the first. he took so much from me that i will never give back. but he gave me so much too; things i will never get from anyone else. a first love. my heart, broken for the first time. a heap of common sense. i hope he will be here. he has a beautiful smile. i hope he will stop smoking, even if you can't get lung cancer in heaven. i don't want him to accidentally burn it down. that sounds like something he would do.

if the second is here, i hope his sadness is gone, destroyed back on earth with everything else. he has been hurt so much. he doesn't deserve it anymore. i know we will never get another chance, not at love, anyways. but perhaps we can rebuild something else; our friendship. who knows? time is endless here.

i know the third will be here, waiting to greet everyone else with open arms. i hope she is there, too, holding his hand. he has a heart of gold, and i am glad he walked away from me without it completely shattered. even now, i would put him before me, simply because i know he is a better person than i have ever been. so if it were between the two of us getting into wherever our afterlife is, i would tell him to go.

the fourth never believed, but then again, neither did i, and yet it is white all around me and i am certain this is not hell. i only hope he is here, too. i promised i would find him. i can only hope i do, and i can only hope we finally get a chance, without miles between us and scattered internet connection being the only thing holding us together.

i think about the fifth, how little time we had. but we have all the time we want here. so much, that one day, we may get bored, as young people do. but i do not want to think about the sad ending now. we have the rest of our lives ahead of us, even if it isn't the way we planned. but things never turn out as planned, do they?

there! i can see them all... they are waiting for me. i must go to them. the air is crisp and the sky is bright. everything is peaceful. the sun will not hurt us here.

here, we have all the chances we need.

-c.h.

Catarine Hancock is a young 18-year old writer and college student from Kentucky in the United States. She is the face behind the famous Instagram account, @evanescent.love, and has been posting her writing on social media for over 4 years now. Although she uses other social media platforms, including Tumblr and Twitter, Instagram remains her most popular and prolific base of operations, garnering an audience of nearly 100,000.

Outside of her writing career, Catarine is an 18-year-old college freshman at the University of Kentucky. She is double majoring in Vocal Performance and Music Education. Her two biggest loves in life are literature and music, and she is thrilled to say she is getting the chance to be successful in both. An operatic mezzo soprano, Catarine is the 2nd place winner of the 2017 Alltech Vocal Scholarship Competition at U.K., the biggest competition of its kind in the world, as well as the 1st place winner of the 2016 Schmidt Vocal Competition. She has also been awarded 3rd place at the 2016 Young Singers Competition and in the 2017 NATS Female Lower College Musical Theatre category this past fall.

Her upcoming projects for her readers in 2018 include the adaptation of her popular series 'among the gray' into a book, as well as a second poetry collection titled 'how the words come,' available this March.

Pages:
Instagram: @evanescent.love
Tumblr: catarinehancock
Twitter: @writingbych
Wattpad: @catarinehancock

about the artists

Brooke Aschenbrenner is a freshman Art Studio major at U.K. She has been an artist for her entire life, and was thrilled to be asked to create the interior art for this book. A high school friend of the author, her art has grown right alongside Catarine's writing for the last several years.

For commission requests and other inquiries, you can contact her through her social media pages, email or website:

Email: baschstudio@yahoo.com
Website: Baschstudio.wixsite.com/arts
Twitter: @artsie_hippie
Instagram: @artsie.hippie

Gaylen Bailey is a self-taught artist, specifically in pencil drawings. He was selected as the cover artist through a contest Catarine held for this book. For commission requests and other inquiries, feel free to contact him via his email.

Email: baileygaylen@gmail.com

33795864R00094

Printed in Poland
by Amazon Fulfillment
Poland Sp. z o.o., Wrocław